The Accidental Servants

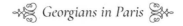 *Georgians in Paris*

Christina Dudley

PROLOGUE

I know not how to defend myself. Innocence taken by surprise cannot imagine what it is to be suspected.
—Pierre Corneille, *Rodogune* V.iv (1644)

Ruin came quickly. There was no note, no whispers beforehand; Eglantine had no premonitions.

"He has absconded!" announced Bertrand, wringing his wig in his elegant hands. "The cash box is gone, and no one has seen him since the first act!"

It was true. After experiencing what was, for their troupe, unprecedented success in Lille, their newly elected company director vanished, taking with him not only the receipts, but also every costume and prop of value which had not been on someone's person, and every script and prompt book not stowed in an actor's locked trunk.

They were bankrupt.

Ruined.

While Monsieur Heine had scheduled a run in Amiens for them next, how could they possibly continue?

"Jeanne! Jeanne, what should we do?" The company turned as one to their youngest member, for what Jeanne Martineau lacked in years she made up for with calm and common sense.

Her curling black hair dressed in a gold bandeau and her dark eyes thickly lined, Jeanne still wore the beaded linen sheath of Rodogune, the titular princess of Corneille's tragedy, a scanty costume which ordinarily entailed being covered in gooseflesh, but on this occasion she was warmed by the bulk of the weeping Eglantine, who played Rodogune's murderous mother-in-law Cleopatra.

"*Sois tranquille, ça va s'arranger,*" Jeanne soothed her. Don't worry, things will work out.

"Why did I have no warning?" sobbed Eglantine, lamp black running down her whitened face in alarming streamers. "*Tout est perdu!*"

"Of course all is not lost," replied Jeanne. "*Monsieur le Directeur* has decamped with the receipts and the salaries owed us, but it is easy to find a new position nowadays. Everyone says so. We will have to split up, yes, but we will not starve."

"But it's winter!" cried Olivier, who had been the Antiochus to her Rodogune. He did not look like he could stand up to a stiff breeze now, much less the queen of Egypt. "No troupe will sign new contracts until the spring recess, by which time we will all be food for the wolves."

Jeanne bit her plump lower lip. Things would indeed be difficult in the intervening months. For her especially. She had no family remaining and had only fallen in with the theatre troupe through sheer luck. They had been performing in St. Omer, where their youngest female actress was jeered and pelted with ordure for playing virgin daughters despite her advanced pregnancy. M. Heine the director tore his hair and foresaw the doom of the company until he espied Jeanne in the cathedral churchyard, beautiful, tragic and unworldly, standing at her mother's fresh graveside. Though Mademoiselle Martineau had no acting experience, she was conveniently penniless and without alternatives and soon agreed to terms. Both the company and Miss Martineau were saved. But now this M. Heine, her unexpected rescuer, turned out to be the villain of the piece!

"We will write the *Juges de la Comédie*," Jeanne suggested, "and tell them of our plight."

"What do they care?" wailed Eglantine. "The royal actors cannot bring back Heine and the money!"

"They have the power to forbid him working again in France," returned Jeanne. "It is small, but it is not nothing."

"It is not food on the table or clothes on our backs," Olivier moaned. As he was the one responsible for Jeanne's predecessor's condition, his anxiety was understandable.

"We must take other jobs," declared Bertrand, his breast swelling. He flung down the wig he had been wringing and looked most majestic, as befit the one who by contract played "leading roles in all genres and all noble fathers." The others halted in their fretting to gaze at him, willing as any provincial audience to believe he embodied all that was wise and authoritative.

"Whatever we find to do will not pay as well as our salaries," he continued, seeing he had their attention, "but it is only temporary."

"How can a village such as this provide jobs for us all?" demanded Olivier. "Heine was due to pay us our fortnight's wages this very night, as well as the week's travel allowance, and now there is nothing!"

"Have you saved anything from your past wages or your advance?" asked Jeanne.

"*Rien!*" he declared decisively. "Nothing. How could I, with a family to feed? You do not understand, having but your slender self to provide for, *chère* Jeanne."

She said nothing, though her lips twitched with amusement. If she had fewer demands on her money, it was also true that she did not share Olivier's taste for alcoholic bacchanals, nor his Pauline's penchant for finery.

"We do not want jobs in tiny Albert," said Bertrand. "Of course it must be Paris. It is best to stay near the *Comédie* players, so they do not forget our case, and we will need to be at the café on the rue des Boucheries for the spring recess to inquire about new roles." He shrugged. "Myself, I will return to service in the interim. To my former household. There is food, there is shelter."

"Service!" arose the universal cry of dismay, as if Bertrand suggested laboring in the fields.

"We, who have been applauded in Lille and Béthune, Cambrai and Arras?" Eglantine protested, thumping a fist to her ample breast. "I commanded three thousand livres in my last contract!"

"But Eglantine," said Jeanne quietly, "it hardly matters, if there is no one to pay it to you."

This evoked another storm of tears and a second draping across the burdened Jeanne. "I cannot! I will not!" insisted Eglantine, who had once been a humble milliner. "It will kill me. Even for a few months it will kill me. I promised myself I would never thread another needle or grovel for another commission."

"You at least can be some man's mistress," Olivier

grumbled, "whereas Pauline and I and our poor infants must beg in the streets."

"Or go into service," repeated Bertrand. "*Mes amis,* there is a time for pride and a time for practicalness."

"Bertrand." Untangling herself from Eglantine, Jeanne reached out to tug at the pleats of his Timagen costume. "I agree with you. Is this household of yours large enough to employ me as well?"

"It is enormous!" he declared, with a sweep of his arm. But the next instant his brow darkened, and he raised an admonitory finger. "But you must not work there. Impossible."

"I am quite good with housework, you know," Jeanne persisted. "After my father died and during my mother's illness, there was no money for servants. I did everything myself."

"*C'est pas la question,*" replied Bertrand. "That is not the problem. The problem is you are young and you are female and you are beautiful, and M. Hubert Tremblay is a cad. A fiend. *Une canaille.* If you come with me, you will be ruined. You will be *enceinte* within a week, and then your belly will swell like Pauline's and there will be no new spring contract."

"Could you not protect me, Bertrand? If you were to introduce me as your niece, perhaps M. Tremblay would not—"

Bertrand shook his head, slowly, mournfully. "It would make no difference. He would consider it an honor for you, to attract the notice of so wealthy and prominent a man."

"And so it would be," agreed Eglantine, now sitting up under her own power and inspecting herself in a small mirror. "It is better for a woman to part with her virtue if she stands to gain from it."

"But first a woman must have some virtue to part with," observed Madame Suard, speaking up for the first time. Though each member of the company was responsible for applying his own paste, paint and pomade, it was tiny Suard who organized and watched over the pots and powders and who brushed and put away the costumes when they were thrown off after a performance.

"Bah," retorted Eglantine, turning first one way and then another and slapping a hand beneath her chin to tighten the flesh there. "Only see what trouble virtue will be for our *chère* Jeanne! She will be afraid even to take a job in service for two meager pistoles a month, lest it endanger her precious virtue. I am glad my father was not a sad English divinity student."

"At least he taught me some English," countered Jeanne, not at all ruffled. "And Papa was not *English,* Eglantine. He merely studied there. But it might help me now. Perhaps I might be a governess. I can teach English and dance and sing and recite Corneille and Racine and Molière."

"No one will employ a governess who has been in the theatre," retorted Eglantine. "If you wanted to be a governess, you should have thought of that before you accepted a contract from M. Heine."

"Nobody *wants* to be a governess," rejoined Jeanne. "I would only prefer it to being assaulted by Bertrand's dreadful M. Tremblay."

"Would you prefer to look like me?" asked Suard, hunching further to pick up the scarves Eglantine tossed down. "Old before your time? Bent? Wizened?" She gave her dry, bitter chuckle. "Because you would be safe from every scoundrel in the kingdom. I may go where I please. I am invisible."

"If only you were silent as well," lashed Eglantine. It was the chief amusement of the leading actress and the company's mistress of the robes to antagonize each other. "But I suppose I will take you with me, Suard. Fetch me those letters from my admirers, so I may determine my fate. Would you rather we go to the mayor of Arras or the lawyer in Lille?"

"The mayor, *bien sûr*! He will know best where to put us. Perhaps near the Square?" Suard tugged on a shawl hanging down to the floor, but Jeanne was sitting on a corner of it, and it would not come free. "Eh? Hop hop, girl."

But Jeanne only stared at her and then snatched at her bony arm. "Suard! You're a genius—*ça pourrait marcher!*"

"What could work?"

"I could be invisible!" Eagerness lit Jeanne's dark eyes. "Bertrand, I could come with you, if I made myself small and old and—and smelly."

"I am *not* smelly," protested Suard, who was indeed known for her dislike of water and fresh linens.

Jeanne squeezed Suard's bony forearm affectionately. "Of course not, dear Suard. But to be safe from M. Tremblay, I had better be. What do you think, Bertrand?"

"Your complexion is too good."

"I would apply the grey paste we use for ghosts and add lines and spots to it."

"Your hair is too black."

"That is easy! A little powder, a slovenly coiffure. Any locks which might peek from my cap frizzled and burned with the iron—"

"You would do better to sell your hair altogether," Eglantine observed jealously. "It is curly. The merchants would pay more than you would make as a servant."

Jeanne merely replied, "*Impossible.* I am as vain of my hair as you are of your bosom."

"And your carriage is far too...springy," Bertrand criticized. "*Trop souple.*"

"What nonsense!" scolded Jeanne. "M. Heine may only have cast me as silly young creatures, but I could have played other roles—"

"Not Cleopatra," Eglantine said smugly.

"Not Cleopatra," Jeanne soothed. "But other roles. Madame Pernelle. Arsinoé. Oenone." She thought she could play Phèdre as well as Eglantine did, and a far less histrionic one, but she was too discreet to say this aloud.

Bertrand studied her through narrowed eyes. "Hmm. Possibly, possibly."

Sensing victory, Jeanne pushed ahead. "And instead of saying I was your niece, you could say I was your aunt. Your ugly old aunt who nevertheless can still sweep and build fires and iron. Better not say I can dress hair, however, for we don't want anyone getting too good a look at me. And perhaps you should also say I am too feeble for the laundry or the kitchen because the heat and damp together might melt my paste. But anything else—"

To her relief, Bertrand thrust out his chest and raised a hand in the attitude of a beneficent emperor. "It shall be done. I will write M. Tollemer at once and inquire as to positions."

"Is it so easy?" asked Jeanne. "Suppose M. Tremblay's household is full?"

"Then we must consult the *bureau d'addresse* for news of positions, or wait by the *petite porte* of the Palais Royal. But it will not come to that, my dear. You will see—in such a place as Paris it is very hard to hold onto one's servants. They are always wandering here and there in search of higher wages or a better role. That is why they will take me back. I worked for Tremblay for fifteen years before I became an actor." Bertrand wagged his head back and forth, taking in the rest of the players. "It is your last chance, all of you. Shall I inquire for two positions or for ten?"

A silence fell as they regarded one another.

Then, "Bah," pronounced Eglantine magnificently. "I will take my chances with the mayor of Arras. But if Suard and I do not like him, we will see you in April at the spring recess."

Olivier sighed heavily. "Pauline and I too will take our chances. She has an uncle in Compiègne who might keep us until then. But perhaps, *chère* Jeanne, you might advance us some of your savings, to get us that far? We have not even enough for the *coche*."

"If you cannot afford the coach, you might take the *diligence*. It is faster, at any rate."

"But the crowding! So many people crushed inside, and the springs so terrible there is nothing to cushion you but your fellow passengers! What use is speed, if you must be miserable the whole time? You would not be so cruel to us, Jeanne."

She might not be cruel, but neither was Jeanne so young nor so foolish as to believe money lent to Olivier and Pauline would find its way back to her. Considering how often the two of them had come to her for these "loans," however, she knew it would be cheaper to send them away to Compiègne than to have them under the same Paris roof.

"Very well," she murmured. "What would you say to five *louis* for each of you?"

CHAPTER I

So may better bargains raise Your ruin'd fortune.
— Philip Francis, translation of Horace, *Satires* II.iii.420
(1746)

R uin came quickly. And if he was to blame, he was not the only one.

"What do you mean, there is no draft?" Charles Ellsworth demanded, his voice hoarse. He grasped the corners of the banker's walnut desk to forestall seizing the man himself.

Monsieur Naret shook out his velvet-trimmed cuffs and rested his elbows on the desk, tenting his fingers. The venerable house of Naret et Fils, *financiers* to the cream of Paris, had nothing to fear from this (now) penniless and insignificant young Englishman, handsome though he might be. And he was handsome, with his admirable build, clean face and bright blue eyes. It was obvious that, before his ruin, he had spared no expense upon his arrival in town.

The tailor had been sent for, as well as the shoemaker, the hatter, and the *perruquier*, for he was flawlessly furnished. For the young man's sake, M. Naret hoped M. Ellsworth had also squandered funds on jewels and buckles and snuffboxes—things which might now be sold to support him.

"There is no draft," the banker repeated. "But there is a letter." Sitting back, he turned the key on his center drawer and withdrew the missive. It was sealed, of course, but M. Naret guessed at its contents from the message to the bankers which had accompanied it.

It was from Charles' older brother William Ellsworth. A man not known for writing, even if the brothers had been particularly close.

His throat tight, Charles slid his finger under the seal and unfolded the single sheet.

12 November 1773
  Symond's Street
  Winchester

My dear Charles,

It's bad news, *old fellow, or so my father and his attorney Darby claim. They say my little debts of honor have left the old man short of funds. So much so that the draft promised you can't be managed at present. How fortunate for you that things are cheaper on the Continent and that this will be no more than an inconvenience, I warrant. If matters improve, we will send funds along. I myself must rusticate at home until the storm blows over. Winchester isn't London, but there are assemblies and such to pass the time, and several rather pretty young ladies.*

Yours affectionately,
William

CAREFULLY, to give himself time, Charles re-folded the letter, running a finger along each crease. This message—his doom—had been written two long months ago. His careless brother had shrugged and sent it along, to sit at Naret et Fils until Charles arrived. Which meant, all the time Charles had been on the road, accompanied by his bear-leader Pocock and his *valet de louage* Dampier, the letter waited. While Charles was hiring a carriage in Calais and following the post-route through Boulogne, Montreuil, Abbeville, and Amiens, the letter waited. In Amiens, Charles and his entourage tarried a full month, so the young man could study the French language with the monks for half a guinea, before continuing on to Clermont, Chantilly, and St Denis. When they finally reached Paris, Charles drove straight to the Hôtel de l'Impératrice in the rue Jacob to command a suite of rooms, with a separate bedchamber for Pocock and a servant apartment for Dampier and a sitting room and private dining room on the ground floor, should he choose to entertain. At three guineas per week it had been dear, but Charles had not known then about this letter. At the time he still had coins jingling in his pocket, and as he could not go about this most fashionable of cities in staid English attire, he had gone straight to the tailor to order new suits, which in turn required a new French-made wig, new stockings, new buckles to his shoes.

But this was not all.

No.

If it had been, even then he might have saved himself. He might have removed to cheaper lodgings and given up the fine dinners at the *table d'hôte*. He might have contented himself walking the city and admiring the magnificent buildings and gardens and bridges and the paintings in the Palais Royal, and so by avoiding extravagance, stretched his diminishing funds for several more months.

But ignorant of his fate, Charles Ellsworth had carelessly trod a far more primrose path and sealed his own destruction.

He raised his head.

M. Naret had been observing him impartially all the while, as if Charles were a specimen of snail. Indeed, the banker must have witnessed ruin too many times to exert himself to sympathy.

"Monsieur," began the young Englishman, "as you indicated, there is no draft for me warranted by my father's bank."

"*Non*," replied the banker simply.

"But it happens that I am particularly in need of funds at the moment."

There was no reply to this, and Charles was forced to continue. "I have, perhaps, been too eager to 'cut a dash' upon my arrival here."

"You have spent money," supplied M. Naret blandly.

"I have. In the expectation of having far more to draw upon."

"And now it is gone. The money you carried."

"Yes."

With the air of one pricking items on a list, M. Naret questioned Charles about what had been spent and where, making recommendations for how some of it—any of it—

might be recovered. But when he reached the point of explaining where to find the dealer in second-hand swords, Charles interrupted.

"Pardon me, M. Naret, but it goes beyond that. I am ashamed to say I have, in so short a time, lost a vast deal at the card tables." He flushed as he admitted it, remembering how flattered he had been to receive Mme de Louviers' invitation to dine. She was the cousin of a peer and filled her rooms with crowds of lofty, titled guests, painted and plastered and rouged within an inch of their lives. Mme de Louviers in particular half-fascinated and half-repelled Charles, her towering wig powdered like white wool and studded with birds and flowers. By the corner of her upper lip she wore a heart-shaped black patch and a diamond one by her right eye. This aggregate of flesh and artifice lured him to her gaming tables, and he, like a fool, played for high stakes. Played and won, the first night; played and lost heavily, the second.

The banker did not acknowledge this news by so much as a flicker of the eyelid, and Charles felt his heart sink to the paste buckles of his pumps. His story was an old one, then. A familiar tale. After all, had his brother William not just fallen to the same fate? And Charles had always thought himself wiser than William.

"M. Naret, I owe one M. Hubert Tremblay nearly two hundred pounds."

The banker drew a measured breath. "The royal tax collector? I see." He drummed his fingertips silently on the surface of his desk. "Two hundred pounds is, as you say, a vast deal to owe. Nearly two hundred louis d'or—more than a laborer's annual wage."

"Yes," agreed Charles bitterly. "Even if I were to retrench in the ways you suggest, it would only prevent further loss. It would not allow me to repay my debt of honor."

"It would not. And Tremblay is not a man to forgive or forget. Compassionate men do not tend to become tax collectors, you might imagine."

Charles felt his face on fire, but this was no time for pride. "Monsieur. Would it be possible for Naret et Fils to make me a loan of the sum? My family's circumstances are...strained, as I am sure you have been informed, but I hope, with similar economies made at home, at some date in the future my father's bank would restore my credit."

Here the financier smoothed his golden cuffs and lay his palms flat upon the desk. "M. Ellsworth, it is with great regret that I tell you no loan will be possible. Naret et Fils has not become the secure banking house it is by extending personal loans to unknown foreigners. But should your father's bank write to us again and authorize us to supply you with funds, we will be more than happy to do so. In the meantime, if you hope to borrow this amount to pay your debt, I suggest you ask among your countrymen. I must now wish you good day."

Charles made his slow, despondent way along the rue de Richelieu, blind to the sights and the beehive-like activity which so charmed him when he arrived. Indeed, he was so deep in thought he narrowly missed being doused with the contents of a chamber pot slung from an upper window.

It was all very well for M. Naret to speak of asking fellow tourists for money, but among the acquaintances Charles had made in his travels, none were Fortune's high-flyers. The loan of two hundred louis d'or would result in their own bankruptcy; nor was his acquaintance numerous enough that he could spread out the pain and request a portion from each. He would simply have to call upon M. Tremblay and plead for his patience. He could repay the man in installments.

Installments for the next ten years!

A frigid breeze rose off the river. Traffic, both wheeled and on foot, was steady over the Pont Royal. Carts of dressed stone for building sites, coaches with liveried servants and coats of arms on the doors. He stopped mid-span to lean over the parapet, his gaze traveling from the Quais des Tuileries to the Château du Louvre and down to the Île de la Cité, before ending at the quays of St. Germain. Tremblay's mansion—the royal tax collector's *hôtel particulier*—stood in St. Germain, not ten minutes' walk from where Charles himself resided. He had never seen the man's house, but when he had lost the colossal amount at Mme de Louviers' tables, Tremblay scribbled his direction on a calling card and handed it to the young man, grinning like a ghoul. "You will call shortly, I trust?"

It was like the issuing of a death sentence. How soon would he care to come by and place his head in the noose?

"Ah, non! *Non!*" The cry interrupted Charles' unpleasant rumination, and he looked up to see a man hurtling his direction, a bundle clutched in his arms and a girl in pursuit.

"*Au voleur!*" she shouted with impressive loudness, *Stop, thief!* Her cap had flown off in her haste and hung by its ribbons, disclosing rich black curls bare of powder which began to fall from their comb and stream down her back.

Charles was not the only young man inspired by her beauty to help her, but he was the nearest to the thief. Without hesitation, he lunged for the man and threw him to the pavement. The thief struck his head on the stones, bewildering him, and the bundle tumbled from his slackened grip.

"*Dieu merci*," breathed the girl, snatching it up and pressing it to her bosom in sweet relief. Then she directed a fierce kick at the fallen thief's backside, following it with a vituperative speech too quick for Charles to follow. The criminal quailed under it, however, and he scrambled away as soon as he could, the jeers of onlookers and a few thrown objects marking his escape.

"*Je vous dois beaucoup*," said the girl, turning now to Charles.

He swept off his hat and made her a bow, frowning as he tried to work out in his head how to answer her. "Er—*je suis heureux—aider vous.*" I am happy help you.

At once a smile brightened her face. "But you are English, I see," she answered him in his own tongue. "My English chevalier."

"You speak my language?" Charles marveled, though he might have been marveling more at her beauty even than her facility. For now that she stood right beside him he could see his first impression had not been mistaken. She was a wonder. Head to toe. The shining black hair was not only curling, it was damp. Her fresh complexion and high color and dancing eyes—either she had fallen in the Seine that morning or she was a nymph risen from her bath.

He took in all these things instantly, in the moment before a curious smell tickled his nose. One which seemed to emanate from the bundle in question. "Curious" was putting it politely. It was some dreadful mixture of onions, perspiration, and old shoes on a hot day, and despite the girl's allure he leaned back a few inches, blinking his eyes so they would not water.

She whisked the bundle behind her back (releasing a

powerful wave of odor with the motion) and dropped it to the ground, her smile faltering. "Yes. I speak some English. My father studied there some years and was deliberate in teaching me."

He would have bowed again, had he not feared being once more engulfed by the stench. "That's—lovely," Charles replied inadequately. He retreated a step. "Well. I am so glad I could be of service. That is what I meant to say."

"Yes. I understood you." She made a comic, rueful face. "And you are too polite to ask, but you wonder what this... *paquet horrible* contains, that I should be so sorry to lose it." She nudged it with a dainty booted toe.

Her frankness drew an answering smile from him—his first of the day. "It is none of my business, of course." Had he known her better, he would have teased her by adding, "I know the butchers' offal when I smell it," but as a stranger he could not be entirely certain she *wasn't* carrying some creature's carcass. He could only think the thief well rid of such a burden.

"I will tell you in any case," she insisted. "It...belongs to my great-aunt."

"Mercy," said Charles, in spite of himself. If such a parcel had belonged to his own great-aunt, he would have rushed out to buy the woman perfume and a barrel of Marechale powder.

"She is a maid-of-all-work. A servant. *Je veux dire,* we are a family of servants."

Charles was already accustomed to the idea that female servants in Paris boasted wardrobes which would have done honor to many an English gentlewoman—this young lady, for example, wore a serviceable but flattering blue wool *robe à l'anglaise* and a cloak trimmed in velvet ribbon

—so her great-aunt must be lowly indeed to claim such noisome possessions. A swoop of disappointment in his midsection surprised him, especially when he realized it was not caused by her great-aunt's mystery bundle, but by the admission of her humble station in life. In England they would have nothing more to say to each other; in France, many men of his class would play the grand seigneur and attempt seduction. But as a friendless, bankrupt, marooned debtor, Charles found superiority impossible, and heartless conquest had never appealed to him.

Like a cloud obscuring the sun, memory of his predicament returned. Was there such a thing as debtor's prison in France? What would Tremblay do to him, when Charles confessed he could not pay? Whatever his fate, he must not shirk it. He must not delay. He must go at once. Or—at the latest—first thing the next day. Today would be spent dismissing his own servants and negotiating an end to his time at the Hôtel de l'Impératrice.

With a stifled sigh, he lifted his hat to the beautiful young lady. "Once more, I am glad I could be of service, mademoiselle, and I wish you will meet with no further misadventures in returning your relative's items. Good day."

Jeanne Martineau (for it was she) watched him go in dismay. So that was how it was? Her rescuer, who seemed as kind as he was handsome, was driven away not by the wretched aroma of her old woman's wig and costume, but by the revelation of her inferior rank? Imagine if she had told him the truth, that she was an actress!

The day which had begun so brightly, faded with this rebuff. Jeanne had risen in her attic garret fighting back the urge to sing because it was her first whole holiday since entering M. Tremblay's service. The garret, drafty and cramped and so low that Jeanne's hair nearly touched the ceiling when it was dressed, would have beheaded her if she styled her tresses over a *toque* like the dowager Mme Tremblay. But fortunately no one expected her adopted persona, the elderly, ugly, hunched, fragrant maid-of-all-work Marthe, to keep up with fashion, and no other servant in the household would have deigned to share the miserable garret, even if they had not objected to Marthe's smell. But it was not just her privacy and her holiday which cheered Jeanne. It was the miraculous sum of ten livres which Olivier and Pauline forwarded from Compiègne. For not only had Pauline's uncle taken them in, but the man had the courtesy to die soon afterward and leave everything to his niece.

Jeanne clutched the coins and shut her eyes, picturing how she would spend them. Why, she would sally forth stinking from the Tremblay mansion in St. Germain, and then, when she no longer feared discovery, she would throw off her disguise, hide it somewhere, and proceed to the Bains de Poitevin for a long, hot, expensive, delicious bath. Ah! It would be too wonderful!

And so it had been. The steam baths were housed in a long white building on a boat near the Pont Royal opposite the Tuileries, and Jeanne gladly paid her four livres for a compartment all to herself. There she donned the bathing garment supplied to her and soaked and cavorted, before thoroughly washing her hair. Sheer heaven. Being reluctant to resume Marthe's clothing, paste, and persona, she squandered another hour walking in the Tuileries Gardens until her hair was nearly dry. It was only when her stomach rumbled in protest that Jeanne slowly made her way back to the Pont Royal where she had hidden her belongings. She need not change her dress yet, but there

21

was a snack of bread and cheese wrapped in a hand-kerchief.

When she saw the thief glance left and right and then bend to reach behind the lamppost, her steps sped. And when he straightened, nose wrinkled and grasping her precious belongings, Jeanne shouted and began to run. The food didn't matter, but she could not—*could not*—return to the Tremblay house as herself. She would chase the man to Montmartre if need be.

But it had not been necessary. The big Englishman had wrestled down the criminal and, too soon afterward, made as quick work of Jeanne's delight.

"It doesn't matter," she whispered to herself. "He was *bien charmant*, but of course he is rich, if he can travel on the Continent. Such people have many servants and court fine ladies. If we met in a drawing room, he would not speak to me. He would not notice me!" She took a bite of her meal and leaned against the same parapet where the young man had stood.

"Still," Jeanne added, swallowing and tearing off another chunk of bread, "if I had been onstage and he in the audience, then *I* would have been the one not to notice *him*."

CHAPTER 2

Fair and flow'ry is the brake,
Yet it hides the vengeful snake.
— William Shenstone, *Inscriptions,* vi.24 (1763)

I n the heart of the Faubourg St Germain, the Hôtel de Tremblay stood a stone's throw from the Abbaye-aux-Bois, where nuns charged wealthy aristocrats hundreds of livres per year to educate their daughters. Passing under the arched entranceway of the *hôtel*, Charles could hear the girls' voices and laughter echoing from the stones of the courtyard and the walls of the vast home itself. The sound heartened him—surely M. Tremblay could not be an ogre when such youth and joy surrounded him.

"Do you have an appointment?" demanded the Swiss guard at the portal. He was a giant man accoutered magnificently with cross-belt and halberd, and Charles hastened to produce the card on which Tremblay wrote his address.

It served, for the *Suisse* gave a condescending nod and

marched ahead of him toward the wide entrance steps. For a moment Charles thought he might beat on the double doors with his halberd (and likely splinter them to pieces), but the man only shifted the weapon to his other side and applied his fist.

Charles' progress must have been observed, for the doors were opened promptly by matching servants in dark green livery edged by gold braid.

"M. Ellsworth to see the master," boomed the *Suisse,* pronouncing Charles' surname like "Ezzwort."

The righthand footman regarded the lefthand footman, and the latter bowed, a gleam of what Charles might have called humor coming and going in his eye. Lefthand Footman turned on his heel and marched away, leaving Charles to follow.

It occurred to him that, if Tremblay never managed to collect the debt owed him, it would not affect him over-much, to judge by the grandeur of the man's home and staff. They proceeded through the vestibule, their heels clacking on the polished stone floor, into the *grande salle*, an enormous space flooded by light. Through the many windows and massive doors along the far side, the formal gardens could be seen. Sculptural chimney pieces anchored either end of the room itself, and gilt decorative details glinted between the scores of people milling here, hoping for an audience. Observing the other callers, Charles wondered grimly how many of them were fellow debtors. Debtors, favor-seekers, politicians, servants—the sheer number of them put a dagger through Charles' hopes. Everyone dreamed of appealing to Tremblay's patience and pity, it seemed.

Two strapping lackeys guarded the further door, and a murmur of resentment rippled through the great room when the footman led Charles through it to a smaller antechamber, one ideal for hosting card-players, Charles supposed from his ill-fated evenings at Mme de Louviers'. This was followed by a succession of chambers, each opening onto the next, each richly furnished, each with views onto the gardens. At last they turned from the series of public rooms into a comparatively humbler setting, a dim library lit by only one narrow window overlooking the stable yard. Oak paneling lined the walls floor to ceiling, and the only bright spots were provided by gilt frames of the paintings and ormolu accents to the wood furniture. A hunched, rumpled crone bowed over the fireplace, tending the modest fire.

"Eh, Marthe," the footman addressed this creature, "*ça suffit maintenant*. That'll do. The master is coming, and he does not want to see you."

"Nor do I want to see him," retorted the crone, rising from her knees with a groan and taking up her basket.

Her movement sent a wave of malodor washing over the two others, a reeky mixture of sweat, onions, and mildewy shoes. Even the footman's professional reserve was vanquished. He coughed, retreated a step, and gasped.

His sharp breath was echoed by ancient Marthe herself, who gaped at the visitor, the contents of her basket nearly sliding to the carpet before she caught them.

Charles failed to notice the old woman's reaction, however, as he was forced to apply his handkerchief to his nose in self-defense. As nonchalantly as he was able, he strode to the farthest possible corner of the room, turning his back on the servants to inspect the volumes on the shelves. He heard the footman muttering earnestly at the wretched maid, his speech low and rapid, to which came a muffled response followed by shuffling sounds, and when

Charles dared to face the room again, the creature was gone. The footman hastened to the window, opening it to the winter air. It might smell of the stables outside, but anything would be an improvement.

Not a minute later, M. Hubert Tremblay swept into the room, his nose wrinkling in distaste. *"Quelle odeur! Bertrand, your aunt deserves to live in the gutters she stinks of!"*

"Pardon, pardon," apologized the footman, but his master only waved a dismissive arm, and the man hastily backed from the room. As Charles had, Tremblay applied a handkerchief to his nose, but no sooner did his eyes fall upon his caller than the servant's offense was forgotten. The royal tax collector advanced, smiling widely to reveal a nearly full set of teeth. "Why, M. Ellsworth! What a pleasure. You are a prompt man in paying your debts. Please be seated."

Charles paled. Prior to this, he had only seen Tremblay by candlelight, and though the sunlight reaching the library was wintry and faint, it did the man no favors. Tremblay was older than he thought, for his powdered and rouged face was lined and in repose his hands shook slightly.

Taking the veneered brocade chair indicated, Charles struggled to compose himself and to recall his Amiens French lessons. For while Tremblay had taken pains to address him in English at Mme de Louviers' gatherings, he made no such attempt now.

"M. Tremblay, thank you for receiving me."

"Of course! I consider any friend of Mme de Louviers a friend of mine." Here his smile widened even further, and Charles was reminded of a wolf.

"Yes." He took a measured breath and then plunged

ahead. "Sir, I will go straight to the heart of the matter. I regret to say I will be unable to repay you promptly. There has been a—delay—in the money I expected from home."

"Ah."

"I hope you will be patient with me."

"Ah," said Tremblay again. "Too bad, M. Ezzwort." He clicked his tongue regretfully. "You are a young man with much to learn. I do not suppose it will mend matters for me to say that it was not wise of you to play for high stakes if you could not cover your possible losses."

To this Charles gave one short nod. What was there to say to something so obvious and so useless after the fact?

"How then do you propose to repay me?" asked Tremblay, his eyes narrowing.

"I—don't know," Charles confessed. "I will of course write you a *billet à ordre* if you like, promising later payment. And I have already begun to make economies, sir. I hope, in time, my family's fortunes will allow them to restore my credit. I will repay you then. You have my word."

Here Tremblay gave an unpleasant laugh. "*Votre parole!* La, you Englishmen with your 'word.' Your 'word' does not pay my bills. Your 'word' does not put bread on my table. Only imagine if I went to my superior the Abbé Teray, controller-general of his majesty's finances, and told him I did not have the head tax he charged me with collecting, but I gave him my 'word'!"

Charles didn't follow this exactly, having no idea what a "*capitation*" was, but he understood Tremblay thought little of his offer. Flushing, he sat forward on his chair. "Monsieur, I regret that my assurance does not...comfort you, but I have no other alternatives to suggest." He did not think Tremblay wanted to hear how he had dismissed his *valet de louage* and was seeking another position for his tutor

Pocock, or how he planned to visit the dealer in second-hand swords M. Naret suggested.

The chief tax-gatherer of Paris rose to pace the carpet, hands clasped behind his back. Thus afforded a long look at Tremblay's red silk frock coat, fastened by a gold frog over an ivory waistcoat, Charles wondered at the man's insistence. Surely the sum owed him was but the drop of a bucket. The candlesticks on the mantel alone would suffice to repay the debt, had Charles been the sort of fellow who stole things!

Tremblay ceased in his pacing and whipped around to face him, causing the young man to give a guilty start. "And you thought you were so handsome and clever and charming!"

"I—beg your pardon?"

Tremblay raised an accusing finger. "You thought to win the heart of my Amélie, did you not, or to find your way to her bed?"

"*W-what?*" blustered Charles, thinking Tremblay had lost his mind. "Who is Amélie?"

The collector colored under his rouge. "Who is Amélie?" he roared back. "She is Mme de Louviers, of course, the one you sought to seduce!"

"I never—!" Charles cried, springing up himself. The man was mad! Fortunately Charles' grasp of French failed him at this juncture, or he would have unwisely added, "That creature? I warrant she's old enough to be my mother, underneath all that varnish." Instead he repeated lamely, "*Jamais.* Never. I assure you."

Tremblay's mouth twisted in skepticism. "You have your pride, young fellow, so you disavow your earlier intentions. I understand. But I am sorry to tell you she will never look at you now. She was not made for poverty, that one, and you, sirrah, are now penniless. You realize, do you not, that if I chose, I could have you imprisoned for debt."

Charles found his hands were shaking, as if the older man's palsy infected him. He would not have imagined his situation could worsen, and yet it had. Not only was it impossible at present to clear his debt, but he had unwittingly compounded the problem by arousing his creditor's jealousy. It hardly mattered whether Charles found Mme de Louviers attractive or unattractive—apparently *she* had found him attractive enough to provoke Tremblay.

Debtor's prison! The horror of the idea made him nauseous. Bad enough to be imprisoned for debt in one's own country. But here, where no one knew him, where no one would come to his aid—how would he ever regain his liberty?

He was at the man's mercy.

Charles sank once more to the chair. "M. Tremblay," he said quietly, "I can but appeal once more to your patience. I will write to my father and to my brother and see what can be done. Perhaps a portion—an 'installment' could be raised." He did not know the French word, so he used the English one.

The note of surrender was the right one to strike. Tremblay perched on the edge of a chest of drawers, crossing satisfied arms over his chest. Again a smile stretched his mouth, but this time at least Charles was spared the display of teeth.

"Perhaps there is another way you can repay me," he began. "It would be humble but honest."

Charles' chin lifted. "What is it, sir? I am willing to do any honest work."

"*Tant mieux*," Tremblay replied. So much the better. "You see, M. Ellsworth, I have two young wards."

"*Pupilles*?" repeated Charles, puzzled. Did he mean students? Was the man an instructor of tax-gathering?

"Boys for whom I am responsible. I do not know if they are stupid or clever. If the latter, I will send them to school in another year, but if stupid, reading and writing and figures will be enough. M. Ezzwort, if you will undertake to tutor them for one year, I will consider myself repaid."

Was the offer genuine? Charles stared at him, trying to discern.

The man shrugged. "A tutor is a servant, yes, but a higher one. You would have your own quarters: a bed chamber and a sitting room which would also serve as a schoolroom."

It was, Charles supposed, a proposal meant to humiliate him. One that his own bear-leader, his tutor Pocock, would have thought beneath him. Whoever these "boys" were, Charles doubted they were Tremblay's legitimate, acknowledged offspring. And if he accepted, he would trade his elegant suite at the Hôtel L'Impératrice for cramped quarters likely in disrepair; he would trade the company of fellow English gentlemen for provincial French servants with whom he had nothing in common.

But, as Tremblay said, it would be honest work.

Humiliating, but honest. And would not debtor's prison be equally humiliating? Granted, most gentlemen would choose debtor's prison over a servant role, but Charles prized his freedom more than his rank. Indeed, with no rescue in sight, any rank Charles clung to would slip with each passing month spent therein. Month? Nay—with each passing *year*.

Tremblay's proposition came with an end date, at least. One year from now the debt would be clear, and Charles might go skulking back to England, God willing, if his family could send enough for passage. In the meantime, however meager and plain, his room and board would be provided, so that he would not take on even more debt.

There was no doubt what must be done. Tremblay read it in his face, and the toothy wolf smile reappeared. "*Ah, bon*. One year for two hundred livres. Will you require a contract, M. Ellsworth, or will you accept my...*parole*?"

The bargain struck, Tremblay rang a bell. When the footman Bertrand came in answer, the master told him, "Tell Fournel to bring Pierre and Georges, with their faces and hands washed, if you please. And then send Raulin to me."

Tremblay's household boasted thirty servants, and in time Charles would know most of them to name them, but the house steward Raulin made an immediate impression. He was a surly, round man, whose wig sat atop his spherical head like a fringed doily on a pumpkin. And as the supereminent domestic of the Hôtel de Tremblay, he was not eager to welcome an English gentleman in reduced circumstances whose rank in the household would be ambiguous.

"Raulin, meet the new tutor M. Charles Ezzwort of Winchester, England," Tremblay said dryly, clearly anticipating his steward's discomfiture. "Unfortunately for him, he is no gambler, but let us hope he can still teach arithmetic. I have hired him to tutor Pierre and Georges. You will take him on a tour of the house, make introductions to the staff, and direct him to suitable quarters."

The steward threw an unpleasant glance at Charles and then bowed in acknowledgement. "Monsieur, there are the nursemaid's former rooms over the stable."

"Those will be perfect."

Another bow. "Pardon me, but there will be some

complaining among the chambermaids. We are somewhat short of staff, as you know, and each is already responsible for—"

"Assign him Marthe," interrupted Tremblay.

"*Marthe?*" gasped Raulin and Charles in tones of astonishment and alarm, respectively.

"Marthe," Tremblay confirmed. "She may be old, but she must do a little more work, or she will not be worth her keep."

So here was another spiteful trick to be played, Charles thought. Tremblay could congratulate himself every day on old Marthe's ripe aroma pervading his rival's tiny apartment, and Charles must either bear it or build his own fires and empty his own chamber pot.

Nor did Charles miss the glee playing over Raulin's features. Was he to have a second enemy in the house before he had even taken up residence?

Tremblay rubbed his hands in satisfaction. "And here is Fournel with the children."

Fournel was tall, thin, and colorless. The fashions of the day required her to wear paniers, which only accentuated her flatness and angles, and altogether she reminded Charles of an upside-down branched candlestick. In contrast, the boys Pierre and Georges were young and plump and bright-eyed, as if they had drained Fournel's vitality and added it to their own. Charles guessed they were close in age, perhaps six or seven, and he was relieved to see they looked lively but not malicious.

After making a curtsey like a brass spyglass shutting up, Fournel prodded the boys forward, muttering through her lipless mouth, "Go on."

With a mixture of shyness and laughing curiosity, Pierre

and Georges ranged a few feet nearer to inspect their new tutor.

"M. Ezzwort will teach you English and arithmetic," announced Tremblay. "And perhaps some Greek and Latin as well." Seeing Charles' start of surprise he added, "Unless you are incapable...?"

Charles thought of the years of classical education drummed into him at Winchester College and gave a nod. He knew enough to keep ahead of young boys, at any rate.

"Very good. Fournel, in two days' time, you will present them at the nursemaid's former rooms promptly at nine, and boys, every morning but Sundays thereafter, you will be there yourselves at that time for lessons. Fournel, tell Marthe to prepare the new schoolroom."

At the name of Marthe, Pierre and Georges snickered and elbowed each other, but Fournel turned a fiery eye on them, and they managed to stifle their mirth, though not their fidgets.

Tremblay pretended not to notice. "Am I understood? Good. Now run along."

WHEN HE RETURNED for the last time to his elegant rooms in the rue Jacob, Charles Ellsworth was a defeated man.

Pocock met him at once. "What did he say?"

Briefly, flatly, Charles explained. He left out the bits about quarters over the stable yard and the smelly old chambermaid assigned him because, honestly, what was the use?

Pocock sighed, sinking onto the chaise. He wasn't wearing his wig, so he ran tired, knobby hands through his remaining hair. "I blame myself, Ellsworth. I should not have let you go to Mme de Louviers' salon."

"How could you have stopped me, short of tying me to a chair?"

"I should have gone with you, then, to restrain you at the tables."

"I would not have permitted you to accompany me," replied Charles. "I was too set on being seen as a man about town, fool that I was. No, Pocock. You have been a respectable bear-leader. I am not the first young man on his grand tour to run into trouble. I am sorry, however, to leave you in the lurch. I think I have about twenty shillings left to me, and you are welcome to half of them. It's less than you are due, but it's something."

"No need," his former tutor dismissed this. "For I have landed in clover, compared to you. Young Lord Thorne's bear-leader has been stricken with rheumatism and wants them to return to Italy for the winter, but Thorne insists on Austria. Therefore I am to accompany Thorne to Vienna. We go in two days."

Charles shook his head, chuckling. "You have indeed done better than I. You will continue to see the world, and there is no danger of Thorne running out of funds."

"This is it, then," said Pocock, rising. "I must go back, and I daresay you had better as well. I wish your fortunes might improve and hope we will meet again."

They shook hands, then, the travelers who had spent the last four months together, and went each his separate way.

CHAPTER 3

Her cheeks with chops and wrincles were disguiz'd,
Of what shee was, no semblance did remaine.
— Shakespeare, *Lucrece,* sig. K3 (1594)

Bertrand discovered Jeanne in tears. He had climbed to the attic garret, poking his head up the rickety ladder after knocking on it to give warning. "Marthe" looked even worse than she usually did, for the grey paste covering her face was smeared, and she was hunched on her cot while still wearing her fabric "hump" on her back, giving the overall impression of a begrimed turtle melting in the rain.

"Mercy. What ails you?" he demanded, holding his nose pinched closed. "And why do you smell even worse than usual? Like a refuse pile at midsummer. Tremblay avoids you at all costs, so I think you might begin to relax your efforts."

She shook her head. "I can't. It is still too soon. The

laundress Dimier told me that monster cornered her where she was wringing out the linens, and he *felt her all over* and kissed her until she could not breathe."

"He did this to *Dimier?*" marveled Bertrand, with incredulity the laundress would not have appreciated. Indeed, though Dimier was a harmless woman and excellent at her job, she was nevertheless shaped like a pudding and distinguished by a prominent mole on her upper lip with a hair growing from it like a flag planted in newfound territory. Moreover she gave off a strong scent of lye, which Bertrand admittedly preferred to whatever noxious concoction Jeanne used.

"He will do it to *anyone*," Jeanne replied grimly, hiccupping back some final sobs. "Any woman. My stench is my only protection."

"So be it," Bertrand sighed, "but you might think of me. It is one thing to have an ugly aunt and quite another to have one so reeking. I am teased mercilessly about it."

She sighed. "Oh, Bertrand, what a small burden to bear! Believe me—it is worse to be the person reeking than to be merely related to the reeker."

There was nothing to be gained by further argument, and Bertrand had a message to deliver, so he got on with it. "Well, I am sorry to find you unhappy," he resumed. "But I came to—"

"What did he want?" she broke in.

"Who? Tremblay?"

"No, the young man. The young man who came."

"He is to be the tutor to Pierre and Georges, and Raulin is furious about it! An Englishman! A 'fine gentleman'! Why such a person would apply to teach Tremblay's two bastards is beyond me."

"Their tutor!" cried Jeanne, her eyes wide. "But why? He

is, as you say, a fine English gentleman. Why would he choose to work, and for Tremblay?"

Bertrand shrugged. "Who knows? Perhaps he has a dreadful secret, for which the master blackmails him. Or he is a spy sent to assassinate him. But most likely he owes him money." A dismissive flick of the fingers. "I will ask Raulin the reason later, but who cares? It only matters that he will work here."

Jeanne gave a little sigh that was half relief and half disappointment. "I see. He will work here, but continue to live somewhere else?"

"Somewhere else? Of course not! He will live here," insisted Bertrand. "He has been given the nursemaid's old rooms over the stables, and I have come to tell you that you must clean them for his arrival. Not just the bedchamber, but also the schoolroom. Tremblay says you are to be his maid, and I do not think he meant Ezzwort to be pleased by this news."

Jeanne hunched even more sharply, her mouth an O of horror. "I cannot, Bertrand! I cannot be that man's maid."

"Of course you can," he answered impatiently. "Don't be so theatrical." It was an old joke of the troupe, one which had been applied regularly to Eglantine. "You think this Ezzwort, like Tremblay, will not be able to resist your charms? Faugh!" Bertrand gave an expressive wave of his hand and pretended to gag.

She straightened, still distressed. "I should never have come here. I should have gone with Suard and Eglantine. I can sew; I can read. I could have been Eglantine's companion."

"Suard was Eglantine's companion," Bertrand rejoined shortly. "And Eglantine would not have wanted you in any case, lest the mayor of Arras or whoever her lover was, fall in love with you instead. Hush now. Stop your complaining and go to work, my precious stinking girl. Who knows how soon the young man will return."

To this point in her life, Jeanne had never considered herself a vain person. Indeed, beyond being proud of her hair, she had devoted little thought to her beauty, except to think how it might serve her on the stage or hinder her in other areas of life. But now she learned the scourge of self-conceit had by no means spared her. Because now, confronted with a person whose admiration she coveted, she realized she was composed of nothing *but* vanity! Had it not been wretched enough on the Pont Royal, causing the handsome young Englishman—M. Ellsworth—to recoil from the foul bundle she carried, but now she must appear before him as foulness personified?

It was too much to ask of any young woman.

In the library she had seen him draw back in disgust from "Marthe," though in politeness he had schooled his face as quickly as he could. She had seen him raise his handkerchief as a barrier. Ah! These things had been as plain to her as his attraction had been on the Pont Royal, when she wore no disguise. But now he could never, never be allowed to see the real Jeanne Martineau again. Not if they were to share the same roof. From now on she must always and only be Marthe Collet, ancient, repulsive aunt of Bertrand Collet.

No, Jeanne had no patience for Bertrand's supposed suffering.

With agility which would astonish her fellow servants, she shoved aside her narrow cot and knelt down to pry up one of the floorboards. From the cavity beneath she retrieved a brown holland sack and withdrew a hand mirror, various pots, a swansdown puff, a silk puff, a powder box, and so forth. Perching by the narrow window through which wind whistled, she hastily repaired her appearance. In fact, to punish herself for her weakness, she made herself especially haggard. More grey, more lined. She re-bound her lustrous hair tightly under an unfashionable low headcloth, pulling out the burnt strands and powdering them a dull shade. She removed her cloth hump and plumped it to greater deformity before strapping it back on. Throughout her ministrations, she resisted the urge to exchange Marthe's pungent shift and stockings for clean ones.

And then, as a final act of martyrdom, Jeanne ate a chunk of cheese pilfered from the kitchens and followed it with a bite of raw onion.

"*Et voilà,*" she murmured, when the task was complete. "I am utterly detestable."

What must be, must be.

Adopting Marthe's hunch and slower movements, she climbed down the ladder.

THE TOUR of the Hôtel de Tremblay which the steward provided Charles had been brisk and cursory. "I do not imagine you will have occasion to be in these parts of the house after today," Raulin told him icily, after they traversed the remaining rooms on the ground floor.

"Does M. Tremblay never summon his wards?" Charles asked.

"If he does, it is before they go to bed, and then Fournel will accompany them," was the terse reply. "You will spend far more of your time elsewhere, hidden away. Let us proceed to the stable yard."

"But what of the gardens?" Charles ventured. "Surely the boys must exercise out of doors for their health."

Raulin hesitated, clearly debating whether this request of the interloper required thwarting, but then he shrugged. "As you wish." Leading the way back to the *cabinet* they had just passed through, he marched to the door which led to the gardens and swept it open. "This will not be the way you take them, of course," the steward warned. "You must come by the passage from the courtyard, so as not to trouble the master or any of his visitors."

"I understand." As Charles had no desire to see Tremblay or the Mme de Louvierses of the world ever again, this would be no hardship.

The gardens were beautifully designed, the formal geometric topiaries and central fountain bordered by gravel paths and encompassed by trees, hedges, and flowerbeds so layered and established that they must hide the walls entirely in summer. As it was, in the bareness of winter Charles could see several glasshouses against the western and southern walls, in which flowers and even tropical plants and fruits throve year-round. The setting overall acted as a balm to his wounded spirit, the more so when Raulin showed him where he would be living.

"We have had no nursemaid here for years," the steward wheezed, after climbing the narrow stairs. The door stuck fast, and he had to throw his elegantly-clad shoulder against it. With a creak and a puff of dust it yielded. "Please," Raulin smirked, gesturing for Charles to enter. "You will want to explore your new home."

The apartment consisted of two rooms: a sitting room garlanded in spider webs which would become the school-room, and a chamber containing only a gloomy curtained bed in which Charles hoped the nursemaid had not died.

On the other hand, the company of a ghost might provide a welcome alternative to solitude.

Charles shivered, and not simply because there were no fires lit.

Tremblay had chosen his punishment well. For the offenses of flirting with Mme de Louviers and losing money he did not have, the upstart English gentleman would sacrifice his rank, his comfort, and all social life. Because it was evident from both Raulin's attitude toward him and from that of the servants to whom the steward pointed him out, that Charles would occupy a social limbo, neither servant nor master.

But it was this very apprehension—that he had reached his life's low-water mark—which stirred the beginnings of rebellion in Charles. His circumstances might be at their nadir, but he would sink still lower if he did not begin to resist the haughty steward. Raulin bore all the characteristics of a petty tyrant, and those who did not withstand him would be ground beneath the man's heel.

Therefore Charles wiped all trace of dismay and depression from his features and turned to regard Raulin with eyebrow raised. "If I am to teach, I must have chairs and tables." He had no idea how to say "shelves" or "blackboard" or "chalk" or "slates," so he ended with a wave of the hand to indicate all classroom appurtenances in general. "And if I am to live here, I must have a wardrobe and...other things for the bedroom."

Raulin raised an eyebrow in return, torn between resenting the stranger's demands and respecting his unforeseen mettle. If he refused to help this Ezzwort, would the master applaud him or hurl abuse? Tremblay was undoubtedly fond of his bastards Pierre and Georges, the steward knew, so perhaps stinting on the schoolroom furnishings was inadvisable.

"*Eh, bien,*" Raulin replied with another shrug, "I will tell Bertrand and Chapone to bring such items. Whatever else you think of, you must ask your chambermaid." He pressed his lips together in a half-hearted attempt to hide his grin. "Your chambermaid Marthe."

His chambermaid Marthe.

Charles no sooner directed the two ostlers from the Hôtel de l'Impératrice where to deposit his trunk in his incommodious quarters, than he tipped them and sent them away, for, though Marthe was nowhere to be seen, her odor lingered.

He forced open the narrow windows and gulped down the fresh, chilly air, though it left a distinct aftertaste of horse.

At least the rooms had been swept and dusted, and the schoolroom furniture he requested stood jumbled in a corner, along with a note: "You may take what books you like from the library for your lessons." Charles had just maneuvered the chairs and tables into position and was considering whether he might use the wall itself as a blackboard when a scratch came at the door.

"Enter!"

It was Marthe. She did not meet his eyes, but she did not need to. Marthe—poor, elderly, humpbacked, fragrant creature—was unforgettable. She was carrying a heavy basket full of firewood, kindling, and tinderbox, and Charles could not help himself—taking one last deep breath at the window, he held it and plunged across the room to relieve her of her burden.

"*Ciel!*" she breathed. Then, horrified that she had been surprised into using her natural voice, she followed this with a series of muttering croaks, indicating with flaps of her hands that he should leave her to do her work.

Charles nodded, retreating to the window, where he turned as carelessly as he could and stuck his head out.

"*Il fait froid,*" she croaked after a minute, rubbing her arms to pantomime being chilled.

Yes, it was indeed cold, and it was stupid to stand there with the window thrown wide when the woman was building him a fire. Reluctantly, he pulled the casement shut. She returned to her work, kneeling before the fireplace, and Charles hardly knew what to do with himself. It wasn't just her powerful aroma—the smoke now beginning to fill the room actually tempered it. Marthe mumbled something, pointing to the chimney, and Charles suspected she was saying a sweep should be summoned.

No, his ongoing discomfiture sprang from his new position. Before his fall he had taken the presence and aid of servants for granted. The Ellsworths of Winchester, while not wealthy, employed six altogether. Food was cooked, fires built and maintained, laundry cleaned, family members dressed, rooms and garden kept tidy, visitors announced. Everyone had his place, and everyone rubbed along. But this—living in isolation with only one old woman to undertake all tasks— this would be awkward. Charles felt guilty just watching her. He might be marooned in France, committed to a year's indentured servitude, but at least it would not be for the rest of his life, and he was straight and hale and his spirit unbroken. All of which could not be said for his new chambermaid.

When the fire was built, Marthe took up her basket again and was going to proceed into the bedchamber when Charles involuntarily raised a hand to stop her.

"Have you...worked here long?" he ventured.

She kept her eyes lowered. "Less than a month."

"So little!" He had imagined her a lifelong denizen of the *hôtel*, like a shade in the underworld. Had her previous employer been unable to tolerate her...eccentricities? He pasted a smile on his face. "Still, it is long enough. I hope you can tell me about the household."

Marthe shrank back, running nervous fingers over the handle of her basket. The motion drew his eye, and Charles frowned in puzzlement at the smoothness of her soot-stained skin. Apparently all the hardship of the maid's life exacted its toll on her face and frame, leaving her hands untouched. Well! Every woman should have one beauty. If Marthe were to scrub her hands clean and adorn them with rings, they might be mistaken for those of a duchess.

"I do not know where you will eat," she blurted. "It will be hard for you."

He blinked. "Won't I eat in the kitchen with the other servants?"

Marthe shook her head slowly. "Of course everyone eats in the *office,* but the *domestiques* do not eat with the *serviteurs*. There is a separate table, but it is for Tollemer—the secretary of M. Tremblay—and the steward Raulin and Montaiglon, M. Tremblay's valet, and the *gens de bouche*. They will not want you there."

"The 'mouth people'?" Charles murmured. She must mean the kitchen staff. They must rank very high, if they shared a table with the aristocracy of the servant world. "Then perhaps—might I eat at the other table?"

This drew an outright gasp. "With the *serviteurs*? They

will not welcome you either. You are too high for them."
She sighed. "I will have to bring you a tray."

"Nonsense," protested Charles. "I must try the table
with the '*domestiques.*' If I do not, both the *domestiques* and
the *serviteurs* will think I am—am—" His limited vocabulary failed him here, so he stuck his nose in the air and
threw her look of mocking disdain.

And to Jeanne's horror, she laughed. It was the merest
gurgle because she choked it down the instant her brain
caught up with her body, but the damage was done.
Ellsworth stared at her.

"Go. Now," she commanded, scurrying past him into
the bedchamber. "If you insist on being treated like a
pariah. Perhaps if you go early, only Montaiglon and
Tollemer will be there. But do not say I did not warn you."

He backed away, holding his breath automatically until
the atmosphere of the room settled again. What had just
happened? What had he just heard? Was he losing his mind
from suffocating himself? Because if his eyes had been
closed, he would have taken an oath he was in the presence
of an enchanting young miss. Graceful hands were not the
only gift bestowed on the crone Marthe, it seemed. He
wondered if, in her youth, when her face was unlined and
her hair not mere straggling whisps—but, no. There would
always have been her unfortunate humpback, and who
knew how long she had avoided bathing or even the change
of linens? It was merely a joke of the gods. A cruelty, even.
To give her lovely hands and an even lovelier laugh.

With a philosophic shrug, Charles obeyed his chambermaid, leaving his small apartment to seek his fortunes at
the dinner table in the *office.*

CHAPTER 4

And a man's foes shall be they of his own household.
— Matthew 10:36, *The Authorized Version* (1611)

Ahousehold the size of the Hôtel de Tremblay boasted two kitchens, of which one was the *office*, a separate room heated by a charcoal brazier to protect precious sugar and desserts and candies from steam. Over this domain the *officier* Babeau reigned, a wiry man with a long, sniffing nose, who considered every servant but those in personal attendance on M. Tremblay as his subjects because they took their meals under his eye.

To reach the *office* from his quarters, Charles crossed the stable yard (with nods to groomsmen and coachmen who did not return the greeting), passed the storage sheds, and threaded his way between kitchen staff rushing hither and yon, chopping, stirring, spooning, serving.

"*Attention!*" roared the *cuisinier*, when he whirled to

pass a tray to a *garçon de cuisine*, only to find Charles in the way.

"Ah, M. Ezzwort." It was Raulin the steward, his pumpkin self blocking the doorway to the *office*. "You have come. I hope your rooms are to your liking."

"Yes, they will be fine."

"And the maid Marthe?" This question drew chuckles from behind him, and Raulin retreated a step to allow Charles entrance.

"Fine as well."

There at the upper table sat exactly those Marthe told him he would find: the secretary Tollemer, the valet Montaiglon, the *officier* Babeau. Lower-ranking servants filled the second table, eating and talking, but at Charles' appearance, a sudden silence fell. He had been introduced to many of them the day before, but that had been in the course of their duties, not when they were at leisure and away from the master's eye. The entire staff was not gathered, since the *gens de bouche* and footmen must serve dinner to the master before enjoying their own, but there must have been fifteen people altogether, and all of them strangers.

"What is it?" Raulin addressed the lower table mockingly. "You have never seen an Englishman eat before? Carry on. When Monsieur goes to the theatre, you will have three hours to stand on the pavement in the cold, and there will be no food for you there."

When Charles did nothing more interesting than raise a hand in greeting, they obeyed, and soon a perfect din filled the room. Every person at the lower table seemed engaged in argument with everyone else, their speech so rapid and colloquial that Charles could not follow if he tried. But he was certain he heard "Ezzwort" more than once.

It not being a Friday, he was disappointed to find fish upon the table, along with a white soup, bread, and a salad mixture of turnips and beans, but he helped himself to all, determined to give no one opportunity to find fault with his company. Not that anyone was seeking it. The secretary retreated behind a newspaper, and Montaiglon eyed him with disdain.

"Where have you sent her?" Babeau asked Raulin, with the air of resuming a conversation.

"Home to Cergy. It had to happen before she could not hide it. Monsieur does not wish her to make a *déclaration de grossesse*, nor does Bastien want to be named, even at the sum Monsieur proposes. I tell you, from now on I will only employ ugly women. It is too troublesome always to be replacing them."

"You have made a good start with hiring Marthe, then," jeered Babeau. "But may I request the next one be less ripe?" He waved a hand before his nose, grimacing. "When that one walks through the kitchens, the milk turns, the jellies melt, the sauces curdle."

"Yet the master leaves her alone, does he not?" Raulin countered. "If Bertrand had a stable full of stinking aunts, I would hire every one of them." The two men laughed, Montaiglon joining in. The secretary merely turned the page of his newspaper.

"How do you like your quarters, Ezzwort?" Tremblay's valet accosted him suddenly. "And your personal attendant?"

Babeau struck the table, still laughing. "In another day or two, Ezzwort will be begging to sleep in the *chambres des domestiques* with those of the lower table!"

Raulin's lips thinned as he regarded Charles. "To avoid a revolt in the dormitory, we have exiled your maid to the corner of the attic. But if Marthe's attendance is too much for you, I am certain a cot could be found for you among the others."

"Thank you," said Charles mildly. "As I said, my quarters and Marthe will suit me just fine."

"That is because the English care nothing for personal cleanliness and habiliment," sneered Montaiglon, running a scornful eye from the top of Charles' perfectly ordinary bag wig, down his perfectly acceptable (though sober) black suit, to his pump-shod feet. "Your countrymen either look like the—how does one say—the 'Puritans' or like footmen for the nouveau riche."

"It's true that many Englishmen would choose to appear serious," replied Charles, his temper rising in spite of himself, "rather than gaudy as peacocks." Later he would wonder how he remembered the word for "peacock" and doubted whether he might have said something else, something *worse*, for Montaiglon and Raulin and Babeau looked like they might go up in flames. But he had been agreeing with Montaiglon! Agreeing that some made themselves too conspicuous with their finery.

Whatever the case, Charles was ignored for the remainder of the meal. He was just thinking he would excuse himself to search for books in Tremblay's library when a light hand landed on his shoulder. He looked up to see a rosy maid—Bette? Lisette? something like that—with a snub nose and dark eyes like currents in a brioche bun.

"I just wanted to welcome you again," she said, with a bob of a curtsey. "Never mind Montaiglon or any of them. They are beasts." This was added in a loud voice, but the valet affected deafness. It was Raulin who flushed angrily. Not that Tonette cared. Her chin lifted. "Only a beast would assign you Marthe!"

"You would perhaps like to be in her place, Tonette?" Raulin snarled.

Her currant eyes flashed at him. "As if you would dare!" Without waiting for his reply, she flounced away.

Raulin shot up from his seat to follow her, signaling the end of the meal. Charles waited for the main body of servants to leave the *office* before rising himself, just as the secretary Tollemer finally lowered his newspaper.

"A word, if you please, Ezzwort."

Though Charles gave no answer, Tollemer did not seem to require one. At his leisure, the secretary pushed back his chair and proceeded into the passage leading to the grand courtyard, Charles on his heels. With the exception of poor Marthe, all the servants of the Tremblay household dressed with style and elegance, but the secretary might have passed for a master himself in his velvet-and-brocade suit and *aile de pigeon* wig bound with matching bow. Charles guessed Tollemer to be approximately Tremblay's age, but it was hard to tell because Tremblay wore thick paste and rouge, while the secretary's skin was bare.

Leading the way to the very library Charles intended to re-visit, Tollemer shut the door behind them.

"You mean nothing to me, young man," began the secretary without preamble, "but the smooth running of the household means much."

Charles bowed. "I am here to work, sir, and have no intention of causing any trouble."

"Ah." Tollemer seated himself before a desk and took up a quill, running the feather back and forth through his fingers. "Your intentions are beside the point. Here is what you must know: the ground beneath your feet is riddled with *caissons*."

Charles shook his head to indicate his lack of comprehension. *Criblé de caissons?*

"There are many...traps," amended Tollemer, speaking more slowly, as if Charles were a dim-witted child.

"Please explain."

"I will tell you of them, but if you relay the stories in turn, I will deny having done so. You are on your own."

What, wondered Charles, was everyone's problem? As if he had come to the Hôtel de Tremblay of his own free will! He, who didn't care a thing for their servant politics or grudges!

The secretary held up a hand. "You have already, in so short a time, made several enemies. M. Tremblay, of course," telling off his points on his fingers, "who did not care for the attentions Mme de Louviers paid you. No—I bid you—let me say all. I do not ask you to agree with my assessment; I tell you only what I perceive. Secondly Raulin, who hates anyone who challenges his rank. And now Montaiglon, because he follows where Raulin leads. Those three traps you might have guessed."

"Are there more?" sighed Charles.

"That depends."

"On what?"

"On your personal tastes and aims." The secretary set the quill down and regarded Charles evenly. "Tonette must be nearly thirty now, and she has a child somewhere in the country whom a local merchant was made to claim in the *déclaration de grossesse,* but I imagine she has saved enough of her wages to make a fine dowry. The master no longer amuses himself with her, so if you would like a wife, there she is."

Charles could only blink at the man's candor, and before he could form a response, Tollemer went on. "She has never liked Montaiglon or Raulin—few people do—but they have both liked her. That is another trap for you."

Holding up his own hands, Charles said, "Thank you for the warning, but I have no plans to marry. I want only to pay my debt, and then I will return to England."

Tollemer shrugged. "Very well. Then beware Tonette. She may use you for her own purposes."

"Hell hath no fury, and so on?" suggested Charles in English.

Another shrug from the secretary. "I am afraid no one speaks English here, apart from you, M. Ezzwort, and the boys, after you teach them." With that he turned back to face his desk, a clear sign that the conversation was concluded, but Charles took his time in going. He had permission to peruse the shelves, and peruse them he would, though there was certainly nothing akin to a primer to be found there. He selected an atlas and a natural history book, however, and though he half expected Tollemer to challenge him when he carried them away, the secretary did not even look up.

Perhaps it was the unwieldy volumes he carried, combined with the odor of stables and kitchen refuse assaulting his nose, but Charles neither saw nor smelled the maid Marthe until he tripped over her. Or over her legs, to be more specific, for she was seated on a bench beside the carriage sheds, eating her meal on a tray. The next thing Charles knew, he was sprawling, his wig tumbling off, and the books flying from his grasp. The paving stones greeted his left temple with a good crack.

"*Ciel!*" cried Marthe, springing up with surprising agility. "Are you hurt?"

Her distinctive scent enveloped him, and the groan which followed was not only a result of dizziness. Charles thought he must really have knocked his senses out because he swore he saw, circling with the stable yard in his vision, a flash of slender ankles in white stockings. But that could not be. Because surely Marthe was a lumpy-ankled woman if ever there was one.

Before he could do more than sit up, hand to his head, a voice called, "*Espèce d'imbécile!* What an idiot! M. Ezzwort, you must excuse Marthe—even when she is told to stay out of everyone's way she is too easily found."

The maid Tonette joined the spinning carousel surrounding him, and harsh as her words might have sounded, her tone was more amused than angry.

"It was my fault," muttered Charles, clambering to his feet. He wanted to pick up the books, but he thought if he bent over he might fall down again. "I did not see her."

"That's because Marthe has a tendency to lurk," replied Tonette, "as if we would not smell her a mile away." She clicked her tongue teasingly as she retrieved Charles' bagwig and the books, placing the latter in his arms before plopping his wig atop his head. "What a shame to cover such beautiful thick hair. You're dark as a Frenchman, monsieur." To Marthe she added, "Trot along, old woman. I will take care of this."

With the passing of his dizziness, memory of Tollemer's warning returned. The last thing Charles needed was Montaiglon or Raulin seeing Tonette in conversation with him, but countless windows faced on the stable yard, and Charles was sure word of the incident would shortly be common knowledge. Therefore he said with more abruptness than courtesy, "Thank you, Tonette. But I do not wish Marthe to go away." When both women raised their eyebrows at this, he added, "I would like her to accompany me. To carry these books to my chambers and—and unpack my trunk—if she has finished her meal."

"I have finished," said Marthe quietly. "Let me put my tray away, and I will come."

With a parting nod, Charles strode away, hoping Tonette would not accompany him. She didn't, following Marthe instead, and he hoped she was not going to pelt the poor old woman with more scathing comments, even if there was no particular malice behind them.

It was some minutes before he heard his maid's slow tread on the stairs, and he hastened to take several deep breaths of cold fresh air before shutting the window.

She was preoccupied, and not pleasantly so.

He could not say how he knew—after all, she was such a hunched, wizened creature that it was impossible to say if she were drooping further, and she always kept to the far side of the room with her eyes lowered—but he knew. Or suspected.

She set the books down which he very well could have carried himself, had he not been trying to distract Tonette from her attention to him.

And perhaps because they were both outcasts of sorts in this hostile place *"criblé de caissons,"* an impulse of sympathy made him say, "Marthe, I am sorry Tonette scolded you. It was my own fault I fell."

"You are kind," she murmured. "Tonette does not wound me. She has suffered much and speaks thus to everyone."

"Do you always...eat out of doors? It is cold this time of year."

"Always."

He nodded, backing away a step or two to draw a surreptitious breath. He was debating.

Well—what of it? he decided. Windows could always be opened when she was gone.

Bracing himself, Charles did the proper thing. "Marthe, you might...bring your tray in here to eat. I will indeed take my meals with the *domestiques* in the *office*, so you will be in nobody's way if you eat here. And then you will be safe from...accidents and reproaches."

Her head sank still lower, and he thought he had made her feel worse, when he meant to do precisely the opposite. When she raised it again, her face remained in shadow. "Thank you, Monsieur. You are very, very kind. But Raulin would not like it. He would think I presume."

Charles chuckled humorlessly, shaking his head. "Does it matter? Tell him I commanded you. Raulin already dislikes me. You had better agree to it, Marthe. Suppose I were to trip over you again? I might really hurt myself next time."

To give her time to think, he turned away and busied himself with turning pages of the atlas. A minute later he heard her shuffling step.

"M. Ellsworth, I thank you again," she said at last. She had retreated to the door. "In that case, I gratefully accept your offer."

He grinned at the wall. But when the door closed behind her, something niggled at him. His brow knit, considering. What was it?

Ah.

Curious indeed.

Because wasn't it odd that, of every denizen of the Hôtel de Tremblay, Marthe alone could pronounce his name?

ONCE OUT OF THE ROOM, Jeanne fled halfway down the staircase before she remembered her supposed decrepitude. Slowing at once, she soon stopped altogether, one hand on the cold stone wall, her breast rising and falling rapidly.

What a good, kind, wonderful man! What had he to gain by showing a repugnant old woman compassion?

Rien du tout. Not a single, solitary thing.

And for that reason, it gained him everything.

She would serve him to the bone, Jeanne vowed inwardly. She would scour his rooms of dirt—she had heard Englishmen valued clean surroundings—and ensure Dimier laundered and pressed and starched his clothing as if he were the king. She would bring him fresh water twice a day and take away his chamber pot almost before he had a chance to use it. He would never, never regret his charity to poor old Marthe.

Biting her lip pensively, Jeanne resumed her descent of the narrow staircase. No wonder Tonette had said to her minutes earlier, "That tutor would be worth pursuing, if I ever trusted a man again." And she was right. A good-looking gentleman fallen on hard times was nevertheless good-looking and nevertheless a gentleman. His kind heart, if others had not already discovered it, would be an unlooked-for benefit, the treasure hidden in the field.

What if Tonette decided she could and would try her luck in love again? With the maid's dowry to set him on his feet again, M. Ellsworth could return to England in a year, taking his lucky bride with him. Jeanne pressed her palm to her bosom to ease an almost physical pain as she pictured the servants gathered in the courtyard to see the happy couple off, Tonette's currant eyes snapping with triumph.

Would M. Ellsworth like Tonette? Choose Tonette? Tonette who was older than he and who had already been seduced by the master and who had a child tucked away somewhere in the countryside? Was that what an English gentleman would choose? Surely not. Jeanne remembered his aloofness on the Pont Royal, when he learned she was a servant.

But that was before he became a servant himself.

Tonette was attractive enough, Jeanne sighed to herself. And her disposition generally pleasant, despite her acid tongue. Indeed, the only people she treated with genuine disdain were the valet Montaiglon and the steward Raulin.

Still, how unfair fate was! If M. Ellsworth's pride had been humbled—if he would now consider a lowlier bride— oh, if if if! If only she, Jeanne Martineau, were able to appear as herself, might she not also have tried to win him? Might he not as easily have come to prefer *her*?

LATER THAT DAY, the laundress Dimier glanced up from the steaming cauldron of linens to see Marthe hunched in the doorway.

"Eh? What is it? The new tutor already has work for me?"

"Not yet."

"Then what?"

"Please, Dimier," entreated Marthe, coming closer. She held out a sour, greyish-yellowish bundle from which the laundress naturally recoiled. "Please—would you wash my shift?"

"Wash your shift!" echoed Dimier. "Did you not tell me it belonged to your mother, God rest her soul, and you would wear the thing until it disintegrated and never, ever clean it, in memory of her?"

"I did," admitted Marthe. "But now that I am to serve the new tutor, I think he finds my odor offensive."

"Of course he finds it offensive," said the laundress, not unkindly. "We all find it offensive. I am not saying I will not do it—I think everyone in the household will thank God for me, if I clean it. I am just asking if you are sure. Your mother will forgive you?"

Marthe put her hands together in a gesture of prayer. "She will forgive me. Please, Dimier."

The extravagant hair in Dimier's mole wagged in approval as she nodded toward her simmering vat. "*Je t'en prie*. Throw it in."

CHAPTER 5

It is a...saying amongst all men, borowed from the French:
Qui aime Jean, aime son chien, love me, love my dog.
— Philip Stubbs, *The Anatomie of abuses* (1583)

Charles awoke slowly to a warm room, the scent of pot-pourri and—when he cracked an eyelid —a glimpse through the half-open door of fresh flowers on the side table in the sitting room. By heaven— had it all been a dream? The debt, the fall from grace, the stable yard? Was he again at the Hôtel de l'Impératrice?

But no. He propped himself on his elbows, blinking, and there were the deathbed curtains, the battered armoire, the peeling paper. The improvements were genuine, but his situation remained.

Throwing off the coverlet, he quickly performed his morning ablutions and dressed himself as best he could without a mirror, making a mental note to ask Marthe if an unwanted one, however small and clouded, could be found

CHRISTINA DUDLEY

somewhere. Plainly, whatever her outward limitations, the fact that she had already made such thoughtful ameliorations to his quarters proved there was more to her than met the eye. Or nose, for that matter.

But when he emerged into the sitting room, Charles discovered his revised opinion of his chambermaid had been too measured by half. Because "transformation" was not too strong a word to apply to what he found. There was the crackling fire, yes. The arrangement of colorful and fragrant hothouse flowers he had glimpsed earlier, yes. And more.

A tray loaded with pastry and cheese and preserves beckoned, the teapot wrapped and still warm. Beside his makeshift blackboard wall, a cup held chalk and slate pencils, in addition to two slates with pencils set on the long table which would serve as the boys' desk. And on Charles' own desk he saw a stack of foolscap, two pots of ink, pens, pencil, and knife.

For a minute he stood dumbfounded, thinking madly that he might weep. Marthe had done all this?

A HALF-HOUR LATER, as he was finishing his tasty breakfast, Charles heard his chambermaid's slow step on the stair. Flinging down his napkin and taking a last breath of unfouled air, he sprang up to open the door for her.

"Marthe!" he cried. "Good morning! I thank you for the food and the flowers and the—" he didn't know the word for *supplies*, so he merely gestured at what she had provided. "Thank you."

She shrunk back, her head lowered so that he could only see the top of her cap, from which the lank strands of grizzled hair poked, but her (strangely lovely) hands took hold of her skirts and wrung them. "You...are pleased?" she muttered.

"Pleased? Yes, pleased. Very much so. Thank you very, very much, Marthe." And then he ran out of air and must take a breath, but he felt such a wave of fondness for her that he did not even retreat to do so. If this good, sad woman was now his only friend, he must learn to tolerate her. All of her.

Therefore, not without congratulating himself on the martyrdom he would face, Charles took in a generous lungful.

Only to receive the second surprise of the morning.

For Marthe—she whose powerful, distinctive scent had nearly flattened him the day before—Marthe smelled no worse than—than mildly unwashed! No worse than, say, fellow passengers in a crowded *diligence* or a goat pen which had not yet had a new day's straw thrown in. That is, while no one might bottle her scent for perfume, neither would they use her as a weapon to fling back invading armies.

Charles stared, bereft of speech.

He was quiet so long Marthe raised her head a degree and cast a wary glance at him. "M-Monsieur?"

"*Rien.*" Nothing. He shook his head. There was no polite way to tell someone you found them less offensive than the day before. Could it be that Marthe bathed and did her laundry infrequently, but this had been one of the occasions? Whatever the case, thank heaven for small blessings.

"Fournel will come soon with the boys," Marthe croaked, edging around him and hobbling into his bedchamber. To his embarrassment, she reappeared with the chamber pot and headed for the door again, turning to say, "Do you not understand? You should prepare. I will return for the tray."

"Of course," he replied. "Thank you." He followed her advice and began to write the alphabet and numbers across the top of the wall, all the while trying not to think of ancient Marthe creeping across the stable yard toward the garderobe. The garderobe which he would make use of as often as possible henceforth, to spare her tasks like her present one and himself the embarrassment. What a different matter it was, to be waited upon by a woman than a man! He stacked his dishes and teacup, scraping the crumbs from the table and transferring them to the tray, before seating himself and beginning to plan his lessons.

When Marthe returned, she found him frowning over the paper, the fingers of one hand rubbing his short dark hair.

"Monsieur—do you mean to wear your wig today?"

Charles raised his head. "Oh! I quite forgot. Yes, thank you. And Marthe, is there a mirror somewhere I can use? One I may have here in my room, I mean."

"I will find one," she promised. "In the meantime, with your permission..." She crept closer to him. "*Levez-vous, s'il vous plaît.*"

As if she had been his grandmother and he a little boy, he obeyed and rose to his feet.

"You have buttoned your coat wrong," she told him. And with only the slightest hesitation, she began to unfasten and re-fasten the large metal buttons nimbly.

"Did you know, Marthe," said Charles gazing down at her flying fingers, "you have the hands of a much younger woman?"

She froze. Even her breath caught, and Charles wondered if he had inadvertently insulted her. He ran over his words again in his mind. Was "more young woman" a euphemism for something else, perhaps? Oh, dear. It would help if he could see her face, but, as always, she kept it lowered.

"It is my one vanity," she whispered at last. "My hands."

"You could have another," he teased, hoping to get over the awkwardness.

Steadily she resumed her task. "What would that be?"

"You have the laugh of a young girl. A charming one. I heard it yesterday."

Somehow he had made things worse. She said nothing, but when his last button was done, she whirled away, stumping over to the desk to take up his tray. So loudly did the dishes and cutlery rattle, Charles thought she might drop it.

"Do you need help, Marthe?"

"Of course not," she gasped. "I carried it up when it was full, you know."

"I know." His brow furrowed as he considered her. "But I would like to be...friends, of a sort."

"*Impossible*," she said at once. "We are not the same kind of servant, Monsieur."

"I know. And I don't mean to upset anyone or anything. But...I haven't got many friends here. If any. No one needs to know, if you don't like." When she did not reply, he added, "I'm sorry. I did not mean anything inappropriate. I hope I have not said something wrong."

Her head drooped lower. "You have not. I will be—your friend. You are a...*gentil* young man. *Bien agréable.*"

If he was so kind and agreeable, why did she look like a dog which had just been kicked? Perhaps he should ask the footman Bertrand about this aunt of his—was her life one long series of tragedies, to make her so wary and beaten?

Whatever the case, there was no time this morning to solve the mystery.

He made a brief bow. "Thank you again, Marthe. I had better fetch my wig before my pupils come. And, by the by, if you ever have time or interest, you are welcome to be here during their lessons. You might like to learn some English."

This last finished her off. "*Ciel!*" she exclaimed, clattering away with the breakfast tray.

The kitchen staff gave Jeanne a wide berth when she passed through, so that it was only Barbe the scullery maid who noticed. "*Quel miracle!* Have you had a bath at last?"

"I was told I was offensive," murmured Jeanne. She knew the best way to manage Barbe was to receive her abuse without resistance. Barbe, who despite her red face and raw hands dreamed of ousting Louise as the master's current favorite, that she might escape the scullery's everlasting dirty pots, pans and plates. But until this could be brought about, she was as barbed as her name.

"Of course you are offensive," retorted Barbe. "Someone must have cleaned your ears first, if you finally heard that. Or was it your eyes, so you noticed at last how everyone runs from you? Too bad a bath cannot wash away a humped back."

Jeanne nodded, taking up her basket of tinderbox, dustcloths, brush, and dustpan, and limping away.

She had quickly learned the routines of the Tremblay household, including where the master was likely to be found and when, that she might have fires built in rooms before he reached them and, equally important, that Tremblay himself might be avoided. Both Tremblay and his ancient mother were slow to rise in the morning, and Jeanne had lit their fires especially early this day, so she might tend to M. Ellsworth, but now she climbed the servant stairs again to the dowager's boudoir, eager to dispense with her cleaning duties. Imagine! When she finished, instead of retreating to her drafty garret or hoping Babeau or Raulin might send her on an errand, M. Ellsworth invited her to listen to Pierre and Georges' lessons! Oh, he could not be as wonderful as he seemed. Could he truly, truly want to think of her as a friend?

It is because he is so isolated, she told herself firmly. *When he is more at home here, he will forget all about pathetic Marthe.* But until that time—might she not revel in the scraps of attention he tossed her?

Jeanne entered Mme Tremblay's boudoir without knocking, never expecting the old woman to be already out of bed, but there she sat at her table, her scanty hair being augmented and dressed by Solange.

The haughty lady's maid rushed toward her at once, flapping one hand while pinching her nose shut with the other. "*Va-t'en*, Marthe! Your smelly self is not wanted here."

Willing enough, Marthe bowed and began to back away, but the dowager said querulously, "*Laisse la tranquille*, Solange. Leave her be. If I am not mistaken, the creature has bathed. Sprinkle a little of my Marechale powder on her and let her do her work."

"Your powder, madame!"

Mme Tremblay arched one painted eyebrow, and Solange reluctantly obeyed, sweeping over to the lowly Marthe and fairly throwing a handful of the expensive powder at her.

Marthe bowed her head again, turning and hobbling to the mantle to tend the fire. In truth she was thrilled to witness Mme Tremblay's toilette because the dowager followed the fashions, despite her advanced age. On went the paste and the vermilion, as well as a patch to cover a pock mark. And then the arduous task of putting up her hair. Solange must apply pomatum; she must comb and separate and pin; she must fasten it down, section by section over the cushion which gave it height and then wind and pin the lower tresses. A thorough dusting of orris-root powder sent a fragrant cloud through the boudoir, and the final, towering construction was pierced by an ostrich feather.

Nor were mistress and maid silent throughout this process, and so interested was Jeanne in their conversation that she almost forgot to keep up her cleaning.

"Have you seen this new tutor my son has enslaved?"

"No, madame, but I have heard much of him. The Englishman."

"And? What do they say? Is he old or young? Ugly or handsome? Foolish or sensible?"

"I hear M. Ezzwort is uncommonly good-looking, but Raulin says he is equally haughty."

There was a thump, and the women looked over to see Marthe had knocked a figurine to the carpet.

"Clumsy fool!" snapped Solange. "That is worth more than six months of your wages."

"*Pardon.*"

But Mme Tremblay came to her rescue again, raising an indolent hand. "Peace, Solange. I should have thought to ask this creature. You there—Hubert tells me he has assigned you as the tutor's chambermaid."

"Yes, madame."

"Put down that cupid and come here."

"Not too near!" Solange rebuked her, and Jeanne kept to the edge of the carpet.

"Have you seen M. Ezzwort yet?" questioned the mistress.

"Yes, madame."

"And is he handsome?"

Jeanne twisted her hands in her skirts. "Everyone is handsome to me."

"Don't be clever!" snapped the lady's maid. "Answer Madame's question plainly."

"M. Ellsworth is handsome."

"And is he haughty?" pursued the dowager. "Or is that simply the steward's malice?"

"He is polite, even to me," replied Jeanne stoutly.

"Hmm...I would like to see this young paragon."

"Madame!" breathed her maid. "You cannot think of going to the stable yard or the kitchens."

"Of course not. M. Ezzwort must be made to come to me." She stepped into the underpetticoat Solange held out for her, studying herself in the long mirror as the maid fastened it.

"How can it be done, madame?" Solange asked. Holding up Mme Tremblay's stays, she encased her and began to thread the laces.

"I think I will tell Hubert that I wish to attend the *Comédie* next Sunday and to take those two little bastard boys as a treat. Of course then M. Ezzwort must accompany us."

Solange inhaled sharply, scandalized. "But Madame! You have never shown Pierre and Georges any favor! It will astonish everyone."

"*Et alors?* I am an old woman now. I am allowed my eccentricities. I will tell Hubert it is because I despair of him ever producing a legitimate heir that I must begin to acknowledge his bastards. Yes. Solange, you must discover for me what will be performed, so I may send the tutor a note."

"Yes, madame." Lifting Mme Tremblay's top petticoat carefully over the old woman's head, Solange permitted herself to roll her eyes. What nonsense was this? Worse than showing those little boys attention would be Madame taking an interest in the English tutor whom her son meant to punish. The household would be in a roar! *Ciel.* She shook her head, taking comfort in the fact that, though this would be the talk of the servants' quarters, at least smelly old Marthe had no one to tell.

To ensure the old hag's silence, Solange craned her long neck to glare Marthe into submission, only to discover the creature had already vanished.

To ATTEND the *Comédie-Française* next Sunday! Jeanne's heart sped. It would be Marthe's day off, just as it was supposed to be M. Ellsworth's day off. Suppose she were to spare a coin for a *place de parterre* and attend as Jeanne Martineau! She had to—it was too great a temptation to resist. The delight of being in a theatre again—with the royal actors on the stage, no less—hardly entered her head because she suspected she might spend the entire performance watching *him.*

And hoping he might see her.

As she climbed the stairs again to the schoolroom, Jeanne heard the chant of Pierre and Georges reciting, and she opened the door as quietly as she could. Nevertheless, heads turned. There was M. Ellsworth standing by his "blackboard," and there were Pierre and Georges at their long table, a slate in front of each of them. When they spied her, they bent their heads together, one black-haired and one brown, giggling.

"Boys," said M. Ellsworth calmly, "Marthe is my maid, and she may assist me in your lessons when her duties permit."

"*Marthe sent mauvais*," declared black-haired Pierre. Marthe smells bad.

"*Tout le monde pense ainsi*," agreed Georges. Everyone thinks so.

"*Et elle est un bossu*," added Pierre. And she is a hunchback.

"Now, now," chided M. Ellsworth as "Marthe" crept to the nearest chair. "I am asked to teach you English and arithmetic and possibly a little Greek and Latin, but I will add something more: *la méthode scientifique*. Can you say that?"

"*La méthode scientifique*," they chanted.

"Good. And under this method, before we say something is true, we must question it. We must observe the facts. We must prove. Therefore, boys, to determine if Marthe truly smells bad, I ask you to take a deep, deep breath." He demonstrated, his chest swelling exaggeratedly.

Still giggling, Pierre and Georges obeyed, their own little chests in their miniature frock coats swelling in imitation.

"And what do you find?"

"That it is true," said Pierre. "But...she smells only a little bad."

"Only a *little* little," Georges frowned. "No worse than the stable hands and far better than the *cour des fumiers* and the man who begs outside the kitchen."

Jeanne could not completely smother her amusement

to be compared favorably to the manure yard and an old drunken beggar. To cover it, she rasped, "Still, it is true I am a hunchback."

But the boys who, hungry for male affection, were already a fair way to loving their new tutor, observed the smile on his face and quickly grasped that the heretofore disdained Marthe enjoyed M. Ezzwort's goodwill. Why this should be they didn't ask, but whatever the reason for it, they were willing enough to follow his lead. Therefore, after studying her inquisitively a few more moments, they turned back around on their seats to see what more surprises the day might hold.

Indeed, it would be hard to say who most enjoyed those first lessons. Charles discovered he rather liked teaching. He liked the boys' bright faces and eager responses. Their curiosity. Pierre was faster to learn the new English vocabulary and conjugation of the verbs *to be* and *to have*, while Georges showed the greater capacity for numbers and addition. They both loved tracing the route from London to Paris in the atlas and the magic of writing on and erasing their new slates. "And when the weather improves we will walk in the gardens to learn some botany," their teacher announced. "Perhaps we may prevail on Marthe to accompany us because she is already familiar with the glasshouses." He pointed at the blooms in the vase. "Could you teach us the names of the flowers you picked today?"

She blushed under her grey paste. Yes, she could. For they had been favorites of Jeanne's mother. *Rosa gallica.* Carnations. Lilies.

When she finished, Pierre informed her with the air of one being helpful, "Flowers are not only pretty, but they can make you smell better."

For the second time in Charles' hearing, Marthe's oddly

girlish laugh rang out, though she choked it back at once and shuffled away from them, grumbling, "What nonsense. I must go." But when she was alone on the staircase, she indulged herself with a long, silent fit of mirth, and anyone who might have seen her would have sworn she almost danced down the steps.

CHAPTER 6

Il est bon quelque fois d'affliger ce qu'on aime.
It is good sometimes to afflict what we love.
— Nicolas-Thomas Barthes, *Les Fausses Infidélités* (1768)

"The theatre?" marveled Charles some days later, gaping at the note in his hand. But there it was in black and white. Mme Tremblay requested the presence of the boys Pierre and Georges on Sunday, accompanied by their tutor M. Ellsworth. They must be dressed in their best and meet her in the grand courtyard at seven in the evening, from which the Tremblay coach would take them to the Théatre des Tuileries to see Voltaire's *L'Écossaise* and Barthes' *Les Fausses Infidélités*.

Had the dowager lost her mind? Not only had Charles never met the woman, but she proposed taking two boys aged six and seven to the royal theatre to see a comedy attacking the *anti-philosophes* and a piece called *False Infidelities*?

He looked at Marthe, who had delivered the missive. Or, more precisely, he looked at the top of Marthe's ruffled cap, since, as usual, her gaze was fixed on his kneecaps. "Does Mme Tremblay take the boys often to the theatre?"

"I have only been here a little longer than you, monsieur," answered Marthe, "but Pierre has not long worn breeches, so I do not think it was possible..." When he said nothing, she ventured a peep at him. "Do you think you will go?"

"Go? I haven't much choice." Still shaking his head, he strode to his desk and took up a pencil to write his acceptance and then held it out to the maid. "Will you return this to her, Marthe? And then I hope you will come back again if you are at liberty to join us in the gardens. The rain has finally stopped, and today we may have a lesson out of doors."

Bobbing a curtsey (which Bertrand would have criticized as *trop souple* in her excitement), Marthe departed, her head full of plans. Which gown she would wear; where she might manage to change her clothing and dress her hair, since she could not afford to visit the Bains de Poitevin again. Could she persuade Bertrand to join her? It would not do to attend alone.

She had reached the carriage sheds when a hand clutched her by the elbow and swung her around.

"Eh? What is this?"

To Jeanne's dismay it was M. Tremblay leering down at her, his long nose twitching. "So the rumor is true. Raulin told me your stink has lessened considerably. This can only be because of the tutor. You hope to beautify your ancient self for him?" He gave a loud, mocking laugh. "Beware, M. Ezzwort! Our antique Marthe has set her cap at you. Ho ho ho!"

His eye traveled down her person, and Jeanne thanked heaven the day was icy and she had donned mittens and a lumpy shawl.

"It is too bad you are a hunchback," he observed. "I imagine when you were younger, you had a very lovely shape."

"I curse you, sir," Jeanne mumbled, *je vous maudis, monsieur* and *je vous remercie, monsieur* sounding similar enough if one hardly moved one's lips.

"Still, I bet all the parts are there, no?" he declared, slapping a hand under her bum roll to pinch her actual backside.

Jeanne took fire at once, and if she had not spent the previous year acting roles, no doubt the game would have been up. As it was, a bellow of rage escaped her, which she then had to mask by doubling over in pretended pain, crying, "Alas! My boil! It is quite painful, sir. I am afraid you have opened it again, and it will ooze."

Tremblay recoiled in horror. "*La peste le coquin!*" he swore, wiping his wronged hand on his coat. "Smells and oozing boils? You should be made to wear a bell like a leper! Why are you allowed to wander my home?"

"Pardon me, monsieur. I go to deliver a response to your mother's note."

This distracted him from his wrath. "What note? Does Mme Tremblay make such as you her messenger? Give it to me."

Unwillingly, Jeanne complied.

"To the theatre!" he exclaimed, when he had read it. "With that worthless Ezzwort?" He tucked the paper in his sleeve. "Very well. I will deliver this. Go along with you. Get out of my sight."

"W<small>HAT HAVE YOU DONE NOW</small>?" demanded Bertrand when he found her sweeping the ashes from the back-office fireplace. He glanced back into the passage before shutting the door.

"What do you mean, what have I done?" Jeanne asked, sitting back on her heels.

"I mean Tremblay rushed into the dining room to accost the dowager—something about the theatre—but then he saw me standing by the buffet and forgot all else to harangue me about why he must employ my disgusting aunt who is not fit for polite company."

"I am sorry for it," said Jeanne, brushing herself off to rise eagerly. "But what did he say about the theatre? Will he permit her to go?"

"What?" Bertrand waved this irrelevancy away. "Yes— that is—Madame told him in no uncertain terms that she would do what she pleased and did not need his permission to do anything."

"Oh, good," she breathed. "I was afraid it would not happen."

"Here I thought my life would get easier if you did not reek to high heaven," Bertrand sighed. "Several people complimented me, as if I were the one who persuaded you to wash your linens—"

"Then, Bertrand," she interrupted, "will you come with me to the *Comédie?*"

"Whatever for? There is nothing for us there. I told you I wrote to the royal players of Heine's thievery, and they merely replied saying they had no idea what happened to him or the troupe's money, but they would 'keep an eye open.' Utterly useless!"

"No, no—not to petition *les Juges* about our situation," Jeanne explained. "I meant, are you free to attend the Sunday performance with me?"

He drew himself up and glared down at her in what she recognized as his King-Pyrrhus-issuing-Andromaque-an-ultimatum pose. "Accompany you to the theatre?" he thundered. "Certainly not! Do I not have trouble enough claiming you as my aunt, here in the relative privacy of the Hôtel de Tremblay? I refuse absolutely to squire you about town—to be seen in public with a hunchbacked old crone who now has an oozing *boil*, I hear!"

"Hush, Bertrand," Jeanne soothed. "I do not intend to go to the theatre as Marthe, but rather as myself. As Jeanne. And as myself I will require male protection. Come—I will even pay for your floor space."

She could see him waver. Truth be told, he did miss the theatre. "But why would you want to attend the same performance as the Tremblays?" he persisted.

"Did you say *Tremblays*? More than Madame? Does Monsieur propose to go now?"

"He does. When he finished berating me and returned to the matter at hand, he said he was pleased to learn his mother would pay his by-blows such marked favor. So, yes, the master will be there. Therefore, should we not go another Sunday?"

"No," said Jeanne simply. "I'm afraid it must be this one. Because, if only for one evening, I want M. Ellsworth to see me as I am, without disguise."

The alarm on Bertrand's face this time was no tribute to his acting skills. "*Ciel!*" he gasped. "Not you too, Jeanne! Why is every woman in this house interested in this English tutor? Mme Tremblay, Tonette, who knows who else? There is no point in him seeing you as Jeanne, Jeanne. Nothing can come of it."

"I know. But I want it all the same, Bertrand."

"Ah, Jeanne." He heaved another sigh. "You are neither my aunt nor my niece, but our troupe was as good as a family—except for M. Heine, may God curse him eternally. So heed your theatre papa: there will be nothing but heartbreak for you, if you love this Ezzwort. He is an English gentleman, though he has been young and foolish, and you are a French actress, beyond the pale of polite society. You can only be someone's mistress, but if you become this Ezzwort's mistress, you would have been wiser to fall victim to Tremblay. Tremblay at least is rich and would have taken care of your offspring as he does Pierre and Georges."

"You wrong M. Ellsworth," hissed Jeanne fiercely. "He may not marry such as I, but nor would he seduce me. And it will do him no harm if I—come to love him from afar. I ask only this one evening to win some admiration from him! A compliment, a lingering look. I will live on it forever."

Bertrand mourned, shaking his head. "*Helas,* the young. There is no reasoning with them."

But he had acted in too many tragedies to doubt the inexorability of fate. Doom was implacable. And if Jeanne were destined to suffer, she must suffer.

"If it must be, it must," he yielded resignedly. "I will take you to the theatre."

"Thank you! Oh, thank you!" She lunged at him, pressing a kiss to his cheek.

"There, there. You will smear paste on me. Go along with you now."

As Raulin commanded, servants were to enter the gardens of the Hôtel de Tremblay via the narrow passage along the side of the house because those in the *grande salle* and other public rooms had no wish to see persons such as Marthe, but Jeanne had not thought to find the other servants clustered there looking out.

"I thought he was supposed to be teaching them."

"Maybe they learn botany."

"It is winter!"

"I am going to join them." This last from Tonette. "Give me your shawl, Fournel. And your basket, Barbe."

"Watch out! Here goes Tonette, to harvest hearts!"

The group startled when Jeanne came up behind them.

"What do you want, Marthe?" asked Barbe crossly. "Stop skulking about."

"M. Ellsworth asked me to show them the glasshouses."

The others regarded her with expressions ranging from skepticism to outrage, but it was Tonette who shrugged. "Well, come along, then."

Jeanne thought the buxom maid would sail ahead of her, eager to reach M. Ellsworth, who stood by the central fountain watching his charges gleefully race up and down the allées radiating from it. But no, Tonette slowed her pace to match Jeanne's hobble.

"You are wise, I suspect, Marthe," was her unexpected remark.

"What do you mean?" rasped Jeanne.

Tonette arched a knowing eyebrow, and Jeanne felt at once exposed. Impossible as it might seem, had the maid guessed her secret admiration of the new tutor? Her wistful longings in regard to him? But how could she? She could not, of course. She would never call such a *tendre* wise.

"I mean I would have said I never met a woman with so little vanity as you," Tonette replied, "but now I see you have vanity after all."

"How could an old withered hunchback like me have vanity?"

"Because you have bathed," said Tonette simply. "You did not mind until now the revulsion your smell caused and now you do. He is a handsome young man, the tutor, is he not?"

"What does that matter to me?" retorted Jeanne. "He is young enough to be my grandson."

"Perhaps. But he is not, after all, your grandson." She laughed, but it was not an unkind sound. "Do not get up in arms, old Marthe. Life would not be worth living if, at any age, one could not dream. No—I like you better now that I see you have the vanity of any woman, along with the foolishness. For this reason, I will praise you, and I will warn you."

She paused in their walk, compelling Jeanne to stop as well. M. Ellsworth raised a hand to greet them, his eyes curious at the odd pairing, but Tonette turned her back to him.

"First: I praise you for your wisdom in making yourself as hideous as possible. Bertrand must have warned you of our master's evil tendencies, and I wish I had had a Bertrand to warn me when I came here years ago. Not that I regret my Lise." Her look was defiant, but Jeanne merely spread her palms. Tonette might have lost her good name, but with a master such as Tremblay, what choice had she had?

"I adore babies," Jeanne said softly. "May she be a comfort to you."

Tonette shook her head, her jaw set. "She is lost to me. I let a rich family in my town adopt her and now only hear of her from what my sister Sabine can learn. Enough of that." She snapped her fingers. "The second thing I have to say to you is my warning: if you have vanity enough to bathe for M. Ezzwort, who knows what more you might do? For no woman could look as bad as you do now without trying. Therefore, if you continue to relax your guard for the tutor's sake, you must beware the master. He is not particular. That is all."

"Thank you," murmured Jeanne, flushing beneath her grey paste and praying no one else in the household saw so clearly as Tonette. "Your advice is well meant. I will beware." But even as she said it, she felt a stab of guilt. Was it wise or wary to appear at the *Comédie* as herself, appearing as alluring as she possibly could?

Having said her piece, Tonette resumed her march toward the center of the garden, toward M. Ellsworth, and Jeanne wished she might speak some home truth herself. What were Tonette's intentions toward him? If Tonette wished to win M. Ellsworth and fathomed that Marthe also found him attractive, why did she not tell Marthe to keep away? Was it because, however much of Marthe's dismal appearance Tonette thought false, she still doubted Marthe could ever prove a threat?

"Good day to you, M. Ezzwort," sang Tonette. "What a beautiful morning to be in the gardens."

He nodded politely. "A little cold, perhaps. Good day to you both. Pierre, Georges, here is our instructress. Marthe seems to know a good deal about flowers, Tonette, and I have enlisted her to teach us. Would you like to join us for the lesson?"

Charles was not surprised when Tonette accepted his offer, and he resigned himself to an hour spent hoping common politeness would not be mistaken for encouragement. But his spirits were not high. If Montaiglon or Raulin were to peer out the windows and see them together, Marthe and the boys' presence would not be enough to make it appear innocent.

When they entered the nearest glasshouse, the old gardener Yves nodded at Marthe. Perhaps because his duties included keeping the bark stove fed and smoking, Charles wondered if Yves minded her smell less.

"They would like a tour of your hothouses," Marthe mumbled.

"What is that to me?" he said, stumping away. "I have work to do. You show them. You know the fancy names anyhow. Only do not let those boys knock anything down. When they are with Fournel, they have never been permitted in here."

"Come, Marthe," teased Tonette. "Don't be shy."

Charles shot the maid a measuring look, for there was something almost friendly in her voice. He was glad of it, for Marthe's sake, and his guardedness toward Tonette softened a fraction. She could not be all ambition and machination, if she took the time to look beneath Marthe's unlovely surface.

"Show us, Marthe," urged Pierre, poking her, while Georges made faces at Yves' back.

Her shoulders heaved in a sigh, but she complied, leading them along the walls and tables where roses and forced flowers and seedlings grew. It must be said that Tonette was more inclined to pick the flowers and thrust the stems into her modest tower of hair, while Georges plucked blossoms to stuff in Marthe's sash or pockets. "Try these, Marthe. You will smell better." With each desecration, Yves looked daggers at the party, and Marthe tried to hurry them along. Pierre listened for a time, but then he too began to fidget until Charles at last set the two boys drawing their favorite specimens.

"You ask too much of them," chided Tonette. "Fournel would bring them to the gardens because she hardly knew what to do with them otherwise, but then she would sit at the fountain while they ran and played and wore themselves out."

"*I* will learn, in any case," Charles insisted, jotting memoranda to himself. "Or how can I correct their lessons?"

"Make Marthe correct their botany," suggested Tonette, peering at her reflection in the panes of glass and rearranging a flower.

"It's an idea." He glanced at crumpled Marthe to the other side of Tonette, her face averted as usual. "So tell us, Marthe, where did you learn about flowers?"

"From my mother, monsieur."

"Did your mother have a garden? Here in Paris?"

"No. It was in St. Omer. I am from St. Omer."

"I'm afraid I've not been there. Is it a lovely place?"

"It is a swamp," answered Tonette. "*Un marais.*"

"It is true there was much swamp," agreed Marthe, "but when drained it is very fertile for food and flowers. There are canals just outside the center because there were many Flemish there."

"Do you come from a family of farmers or florists, then?"

"No. Neither. My father was a master at the Jesuit

college before he...died. Most of the college is no longer there. It moved to Bruges, I think. But to become a master, he studied in England for a time."

"Did he?" cried Charles, pleased. "He must have learned some English, then. Do you know, you are the second person I've met in Paris whose father studied in England? I had no idea my country was so popular for study among Catholics. Did he teach you any?"

"Yes, a little." Jeanne thought her knees would buckle. *Idiot!* How could she have forgotten having told M. Ellsworth about Papa studying in England?

"That is why you can pronounce 'Ellsworth,'" he chuckled. "How utterly unexpected. But our countries have been so often at war—when was he in England?"

She tried to arrest her racing thoughts. Because she expected no one to take any interest in Marthe's history, she and Bertrand had not bothered to invent one for her. And now she had blundered and told M. Ellsworth the truth—the same story Jeanne told on the Pont Royal!

Oh, dear.

But what was done was done. She must simply make the best of it.

It was absolutely true England and France had been at war frequently—how old was Marthe supposed to be? And how old would that make Marthe's father?

"I do not know," she blurted. "He died when I was very, very, very young."

"In the days of Charlemagne, it sounds like," interposed Tonette wryly.

Charles frowned. "If you were so very young, it's a wonder you recall *any* English words."

"I don't," she said hastily. "I do not know why I said that. It was—it was a lie."

"Oh la, monsieur," cooed Tonette mischievously. "How can you be surprised, when you have heard Marthe recite these Latin plant names? Clearly she is a woman of many *hidden* talents. But have pity if she told a little lie. It is your handsome face and straight shoulders which make *all* of us want to impress you. Marthe especially because she is so charmingly crooked."

"It is true," agreed Jeanne, now eager for the overly observant Tonette to shut up as well. "You have very straight shoulders, monsieur. Like—like my father. He would carry me on them. But please—let us not talk anymore about me or him. Very sad."

Thus ended the botany lesson, and Jeanne could not help but think that, of them all, it was Tonette who had learned the most.

CHAPTER 7

On the stage he was natural, simple, affecting,
'Twas only that, when he was off, he was acting.
— Oliver Goldsmith, "Retaliation" (1774)

"Have you lost your mind?" cried Bertrand, when Jeanne emerged into the smoky foyer of the Théatre des Tuileries. He had, by dint of putting the screws to one of the underlings who owed him favors from long ago, secured her a small closet in which to effect her transformation. And though he had been prepared to see the old Jeanne Martineau for the first time in weeks, this—!

"Is something amiss?" she fretted. "It is no easy task to dress my own hair in a dark little space full of spiders!"

"You are—breathtaking, *ma chère*," he sighed, shaking his head as he studied her. It was true that her hair was not as high as was fashionable, and her powder uneven so that black peeked through in places. It was true as well that she had no newer or nicer gown than the dark blue wool *robe à l'anglaise,* which was not fine enough for the theatre. But none of that mattered. She was young and fresh and the color in her cheeks owed nothing to rouge, nor the brightness in her eyes to belladonna. "The problem is that no one will believe I have been hiding a niece in Paris who looks like you!"

"Why can I not be your niece? Your niece in service for a petty bourgeois family in the Marais."

"Why would I find employment for my aged, reeking aunt, and not for my niece?" Bertrand countered.

"Because I had no need of employment," answered Jeanne. "I was already employed. And *I* could not find places for you and your aunt because my master is not rich enough to need so many, and old Marthe Collet would not be hired apart from you. But no one will ask these things, Bertrand!"

"That is not all, Jeanne," he scolded. "The crowd in the *parterre* can be rough. Even with me beside you, it would be better to draw no attention to yourself."

"Nor will I!"

His only reply was a groan, and she lost patience. "Come, you sound like an old woman. Let us find a place."

Whatever Bertrand's misgivings, Jeanne's only fear was that they would not be able to see the Tremblay party. Then, as both the pit and the loges began to fill, she feared the Tremblays would not attend at all. Her gaze swept the boxes again. It would not be a problem of failing to recognize them, surely, though neither she nor Bertrand owned an opera-glass. Who else would come to the theatre accompanied by two young boys?

By the time the first play began, Jeanne and Bertrand were hemmed in by hundreds of others: artisans, students, laborers, journalists, prostitutes. No noticeable diminution of noise or activity followed the entrance of the actors, and they were forced to bellow into the vast space. Jeanne drooped abjectly against Bertrand, fighting tears in her disappointment. She hardly cared that several men were casting her bold looks which she ordinarily would have resented.

But then—behold!—through the haze thrown by the profusion of candles appeared new persons, making their way to one of the four boxes built upon the stage itself. Jeanne's breath caught to see M. Ellsworth in his finery. A scarlet coat and breeches with linen shirt and ivory waistcoat, and how fine a figure he cut! And how perfect that Mme Tremblay secured so conspicuous a place, even if M. Ellsworth and his two charges sat behind the master and the dowager. Jeanne might watch the Englishman to her heart's content, with no one being the wiser. But how could she ever attract *his* attention in the crammed pit?

She was unexpectedly helped by one of the overbold young men Bertrand frowned on earlier, one who must have imbibed freely before the performance and who was egged on by his friends.

"Ma'm'selle," came his slurred address, in the momentary lull following a ripple of audience laughter. "What are you doing at the theatre with this old man, when you might have a young one like me? The month of May should have nothing to do with December."

"December is my uncle," Jeanne said with a toss of her head, turning her back on him.

The man's friends jeered at him for this rebuff, one of them thrusting him forward again. Giving a tug on her skirts, the drunk man swept off his hat and bowed, bumping several people behind him with his backside. "If December is your uncle, may I then suggest *July* as your lover?"

With a flash of her eyes, she whisked her gown from his grasp. "With such puerile conduct, sirrah, I took you for March."

His fellows roared with laughter, but before the drunken man's addled mind could retort on her, those whom his hind end had inconvenienced took their revenge, giving him a mighty shove that hurled him head foremost into Jeanne, and she into Bertrand. Down went the threesome with screams and bellows.

Even such seasoned performers as the *comedians du roi* could not ignore such a fracas, and the action on the stage halted momentarily. The drunken man sprang up again, staggering about and cursing volubly, and he would have flung himself upon the offenders, had not his friends taken him up. Others in the *parterre* shouted upon him to shut his mouth or get out, so they could watch the show, sentiments which rankled the drunken man's friends, and a thorough-going row might have broken out, had the guards not marched in and hauled away a fair lot of them. Meanwhile, pockets were picked, things were thrown in indignation, and everyone's shouts were lost in the din of everyone else's.

"Come, Bertrand," hissed Jeanne, in the uproar. Seizing his arm, she took advantage of the commotion to squeeze their way forward. With any luck, M. Ellsworth had not yet seen her, and she might try again to make a pleasing impression on him.

BUT BOTH BERTRAND and Jeanne had indeed been noticed.

"*Quel tumulte,*" murmured Mme Tremblay, training her opera-glass on the pit. "I declare, it is worse every time I come."

"They speak of putting benches in," her son replied, raising his own glass. "Sitting down is halfway to falling asleep. Ezzwort, do they not have benches in the pit in Lon—" He broke off halfway through his question, leaning forward. "I say! What a lovely creature."

"Where?" His mother lowered her glass to see where he pointed and then scanned the crowd again. "Oh, la! If you were not so busy looking at the girl, you would notice something about her companion."

"What about him?"

"*Idiot!* If I am not mistaken, does he not work in our home?"

Tremblay scoffed. "One wigged footman is indistinguishable from another. Why should I pay attention to any of them?"

"I thought you said the girl was pretty," Mme Tremblay replied. "Would you not like to know how to find her?" Looking over her shoulder she added, "Here, M. Ezzwort. You look and tell me if that is not one of our servants. The ones there—they are moving."

Dutifully, Charles put the opera-glass to his eye, ignoring Pierre plucking at his sleeve and whispering, "May I see, monsieur? May I?"

Charles' breath caught as sharply as Tremblay's had, but for entirely different reasons. For it was she—the girl from the Pont Royal! It could be no other—the blue dress, the dark eyes, the curling hair. Being thrown to the ground, she had lost a comb from her coiffure, and a lock of rippling powder-and-black ran down her back. Oh, yes, he remembered her. The nymph from the Seine.

"Am I not right?" prompted Mme Tremblay, recalling him. "Perhaps you might even know his name."

Hastily, Charles ran the glass along the girl's arm to see the man she clung to. And— "Yes," he said, amazed. "It is— Bertrand. One of the footmen. You have a keen eye, madam. I would not have picked him out when he is not in livery."

"There!" declared Mme Tremblay triumphantly. "I told you, Hubert. Well—now you know where to find her. You need only ask this Bertrand. I suppose within the week this girl will be underfoot. But I warn you: it will create a fuss with whoever it is you are carrying on with now. What was her name?"

He shrugged. "I can get rid of the other." He glanced at Charles. "At the interval, you go down there and buy sweets for the boys and find out what you can about Bertrand's little beauty."

It was a commission Charles was quite willing to undertake, if only to warn them of Tremblay's designs.

Once the troublemakers were escorted from the pit, the play resumed, though in truth not everyone in their box gave it his full attention. The boys at least were rapt from the novelty of the experience, and Mme Tremblay always enjoyed her Voltaire, but Charles observed her son's glass rarely left his eye, and when it was raised it was fixed on Bertrand and the girl. Having given back the dowager's glass, Charles could not see the young lady as clearly as he wished, but he too watched her more than he did the actors.

At last, the Scotsman Monrose's desire to "avenge by the blood of the son all the barbarities of the father" yielded to his daughter's love for that same son, and harmony was restored. The constant buzz of the *parterre* turned to applause, but the lowering of the chandeliers to replace the candles signaled the interval, and the audience began to move in restless waves. Those in the pit went in search of food, drink, and mischief, while those in boxes slipped out to visit others or prepared themselves to receive.

Charles managed to escape the Tremblays' loge just before the first party arrived, and he was glad to see ladies among the group, for he hoped to speak with Bertrand and the girl without Tremblay's eye fastened on them. If only they did not vanish before he could make his way down!

They did not. Jeanne in fact took firm hold of Bertrand, urging, "We must stay exactly here." Through the smoky air she had glimpsed how often M. Ellsworth's face drifted to the pit, but she could not tell if it was mere woolgathering. Alas, the gleam of the opera-glass in M. Tremblay's hand made it too clear that he looked her way deliberately, but Jeanne could not spare him more than a flicker or two of annoyance.

Her heart raced when she discovered M. Ellsworth gone from the Tremblay loge, but she willed herself not to look around. *Please please please—*

"Good evening, Bertrand."

Jeanne thought she could feel the rumble of his low voice in every fiber of her person. She clutched Bertrand's arm even tighter until he raised his brows at her and hissed, "Have pity on the circulation of my blood." Then, "Good evening, M. Ezzwort. You are very prominent on the stage. I saw you and the Tremblays at once."

"Yes. I don't believe I've ever been so close to the actors," Charles answered vaguely. "I did see you had a little disturbance here. I hope you and the young lady were not injured."

"Yes, the young lady," said Bertrand with an affected start of surprise. "Do allow me to introduce my niece Miss Martineau. Jeanne, this is M. Ezzwort, the tutor for the wards of Tremblay."

Jeanne raised her dark eyes to the young man's, and it was a wonder neither of them fell down.

"I...have met Miss Martineau," Charles managed to say, when Miss Martineau said nothing at all. "If you remember —perhaps a fortnight ago on the Pont Royal. Your bundle. It was taken."

"Ah, but yes, I remember," breathed Jeanne.

Bertrand tried unobtrusively to pull away from her grip because his fingers were going numb.

"Or perhaps I should say, your great-aunt's bundle," Charles added. His brow creased as his mind caught up to what Bertrand had just told him. "Wait a moment— Bertrand, did you say Miss Martineau here is your niece?"

"Yes. Niece."

"And have you not also told me my chambermaid Marthe Collet is your aunt?"

"Yes..."

"Then—" his features lit with a sudden smile "—then Miss Martineau, I know your great-aunt, whose bundle we saved! She is my kindly chambermaid. Why, what a marvelous coincidence! Wonderful. I am more than delighted both to meet with you again and to learn your name. And I hope my French has improved since we last met—it makes a difference that I now have no one with whom to speak English."

"You don't?" asked Jeanne. (She would kick herself later

for such a witless response, but he did not seem disgusted by it.)

"Not a single soul," he replied with a grin. "But how glad I am you remember me! Though perhaps you will want to shun my acquaintance when I tell you more of my story. You met me for the first time on a very sad occasion, I'm afraid. You see—as I'm sure your uncle can explain to you—I found myself quite short of funds that day. Not just that day, but that was when I learned of it. I had just come from speaking with the banker. Anyway, to make a long story short, I have now through this position at the Hôtel de Tremblay an opportunity to pay my debts. All of which is to say, I was distracted when we first met." He was babbling, he knew, and abruptly shut his mouth.

She glowed up at him. "Monsieur, I found no fault with you that day, and I rejoice to hear that you have found a means to discharge your debt. And—and I am glad to learn as well that my great-aunt Marthe can be of service to you."

"Oh, she's a treasure! She has cleaned and brightened my quarters and is so willing to help when I ask. Many mornings when she has time, she sits in the schoolroom while my pupils learn, and she even taught us some botany. I will value her all the more, mademoiselle, with your permission, now that I know she counts among her virtues such a—charming—family member. Family members, that is," he added, belatedly remembering Bertrand's presence. The footman merely rolled his eyes.

"My—great-aunt Marthe must surely delight in serving you, Monsieur," returned Jeanne. "So—pleasant and—thoughtful a person."

"I would like some refreshments," announced Bertrand. "If only my fingers were still capable of beckoning to the vendors."

Neither Charles nor Jeanne heard him.

"Do you ever visit your great-aunt?" he asked her.

Her eyes widened. "I-I-I—no, I don't." The bald answer puzzled him, and she hastened on. "Because—she warned me about M. Tremblay. Otherwise I would. But both she and my uncle have told me never to show my face there."

"Good heavens!" cried Charles in English, at last recalling the warning he had intended to deliver. "That's right. I meant to say. You had better stay far away from us. It's no place for a respectable young lady. You are far better off where you are. Wherever that is."

"The Marais," said Jeanne. "I work for a bourgeois family there."

"Good. Far from danger, I hope. But perhaps—you might like to see your great-aunt. I could accompany her to visit you next Sunday, if you both would like."

Jeanne felt as if an iron band had been fastened around her breast, and she hardly knew whether joy or dismay was uppermost. He not only had noticed her—he *liked* her! He would like to see her again, despite her being a servant! Ah, if only it were possible.

Oh, what should she do? Undeceive him immediately about Marthe's identity? But if she did, she could not possibly continue in his company as Marthe every day. In fact, she could not possibly continue at the Hôtel de Tremblay, and then what would become of her?

"*Impossible*," she declared aloud. "I—am not allowed to receive visitors."

He drew back, abashed. "Or we could walk in the Tuileries—Marthe and you and I, if you would prefer, mademoiselle."

"*Impossible*," repeated Jeanne, panic rising. But what excuse could she give to fend off such an innocuous suggestion? "My—my great-aunt does not like outings. Her—strength is not—she is not fit for it."

At this a shadow crossed his features. Had he misread her? Did she not want to become better acquainted? He did not think he deceived himself that she had been pleased to see him again.

But the other possible explanation made him almost as unhappy.

Could it be that the pretty Miss Martineau was ashamed to be seen in public with her elderly relation? Most young ladies would shrink from inviting sad Marthe to accompany them, Charles hastened to make excuses for her. Of course they would. Indeed, from the way Marthe had smelled until very recently, *everyone* had shrunk from spending time with her. Every last person at the Hôtel de Tremblay. Even Bertrand was seen with his aunt as little as possible. It was perfectly understandable. And he, Charles, need not think himself virtuous simply because he had come to appreciate his chambermaid. Had they not been forced into each other's company, it might never have come about.

All the same, even as he justified the young lady to himself, he was aware of faint disappointment. As someone himself far from home and family, Charles thought it regrettable Miss Martineau disdained any relative, however humble.

"But perhaps my uncle Bertrand would come with us," suggested Jeanne eagerly.

Bertrand had only begun to sputter in response when Charles answered, "I am sure he is a busy man on his rest days." He was also sure that what might be considered a treat for Marthe would be a burden for Bertrand. And how would walking with Bertrand help bring Marthe and her great-niece together? Perhaps what Charles ought to do was sound Marthe on her relationship with her great-niece. Did Marthe feel affection for her? Could Marthe be persuaded to spruce herself up further, so that Miss Martineau would not hesitate to be seen with her? Time would tell.

"Ah," he said. "They have replaced the candles, and the next performance will begin shortly. It was a great pleasure to make your acquaintance, Miss Martineau, and I hope circumstances will allow us to meet again in the future."

He was going to go, with nothing resolved? "I might—come to see my uncle and great-aunt after all," blurted Jeanne, desolated by his withdrawal. "And surely I would see you then."

But instead of appearing delighted by this proposal, his face grew suddenly stern. "I would not recommend it, Miss Martineau. Because unfortunately your uncle is right. Our home is no safe place for—such as you. I bid you good evening."

Jeanne could have cried, to see him turn and go, but her hold of Bertrand's arm loosened, and the man uttered an oath and ripped himself free. "*Grâce à Dieu*," he muttered, "Soon they would have had to amputate."

"Oh, Bertrand, why did you hesitate when he said you might chaperone us on a walk?"

"Because you have taken leave of your senses, Jeanne! Nothing can come of this," he argued. "Even if we were to say Marthe died and we tossed her body in the Seine, you could not marry this man or even be his mistress because he hasn't an *eçu* that does not belong to Tremblay." Her head bowed, but he must hammer on—for her own good. "Where would you live? *How* would you live? You could find another position, yes, but he will not leave his post because there would still be the debt to be paid." He reached for her hand to pat it. "Oh, come now, do not weep, *chèrie*. You are young. Soon you will be on the stage again like these marvelous actors, and you will forget all about this impoverished Englishman. Let us enjoy *Les Fausses Infidélités*. If we like it enough, we can suggest it to our next troupe..."

CHAPTER 8

L'amour rend des femmes discrètes.
Je vais mener de front deux intrigues sécretes.
Love makes women discreet.
I will engage in secret intrigues.
— Nicolas-Thomas Barthes, *Les Fausses Infidélités* (1774)

"*Et alors?*" drawled Tremblay, when Charles returned to the box. "What did you discover, my English spy?"

Before replying, Charles distributed to the boys the biscuits and oranges he had purchased at the last minute. "The man was indeed your servant Bertrand and the girl his niece."

"Niece!" laughed Mme Tremblay. "That man fills Paris with his female relations." She rapped her son with her fan. "You need not tell me, Hubert. I suppose you want me to dismiss my Solange so that we may take the niece on? She does not look so dexterous at hair-dressing, to judge from her own coiffure, but I daresay she will improve with practice."

"Pardon me, madame," interposed Charles, "but she is already employed with a bourgeois family in the Marais."

Tremblay shrugged. "We will ask Bertrand her wages. Everyone has his price."

To Charles' relief, the second play of the program began, and this time he was not left much to his own thoughts because Pierre and Georges grew restless, whispering questions to him about the characters and the plot and why Dorimène and Angélique were pretending to love someone else and whether he thought those who tended the theatre candles ever swung from the chandelier. At some point during all this, Bertrand and his niece slipped away, for when Charles looked again for them, they were gone. His heart sank a little; he would have liked to pick out Miss Martineau's outline, even if he could not see her clearly, and even if she chose to forego Charles' company rather than be seen walking in the Tuileries with her great-aunt.

I will ask Marthe about her, he told himself again. That would be a pleasure in itself, to talk about Miss Martineau with others. And perhaps, if there were some way to make Marthe more presentable, Miss Martineau might change her mind about being seen in her presence. She might even come to appreciate the old woman's hidden merits. It would be a good deed on Charles' part—a good deed which paid its own rewards.

CHARLES ELLSWORTH WAS NOT the only one making plans.

Jeanne lay awake in her drafty garret that night,

thinking and thinking. Oh—here was a pretty kettle of fish, indeed! What could be done? Could anything be done? It was all very well for Bertrand to tell her to forget about the Englishman—Bertrand who claimed only ever to have cared for his long-dead wife. "But it was tragedy which honed my craft!" he had often declared to their troupe. "If you have never suffered a broken heart, you will never play anything well but comedic roles." To which Eglantine retorted, "I have suffered ten times the tragedies you have, Bertrand. Therefore the real marvel is that I am still such a magnificent *comédienne*."

No—Bertrand could not understand because he was no longer a young man. His blood did not flow hot in his veins anymore. His heart did not pound and beg for release when he cared too much for someone or something. He might summon tears and anguish when treading the stage as Pyrrhus or Pompée, but once the scenes ended he was tranquil enough.

All Jeanne knew was that she could not simply leave matters as they were. She could not simply disappear again into Marthe, never to try again to charm M. Ellsworth. It was not as hopeless as Bertrand insisted! It could not be. M. Ellsworth would be free in a year, after all, and then she might follow him if she could, wherever he chose to go, if he would have her.

When she rose early the following morning, she had no plan. There had been no bolt of lightning to illuminate her path. She only knew she could not bear to be Marthe this day, in all Marthe's repulsiveness.

She could not bear to put on even a mildly odorous shift or petticoat and reached instead under the floorboard for a clean one, hoping the lavender she had packed it with would not be too obvious.

Nor could she bring herself to apply the grey paste in its usual thickness. She might scrimp a little, she told herself. She would keep her head down. No one looked at Marthe anyway. And for these same reasons, she drew fewer and lighter lines across her forehead, flanking her mouth, and radiating from her eyes.

She could not leave off her hump altogether, however, nor even reduce its size, for it was indeed but half of a bum roll—a stuffed cushion with straps sewn on. Perhaps tonight she could open the seam and pull out some of the padding.

And her hair—here Jeanne was most reckless of all. With a tiny pair of scissors she snipped off the burnt and grizzled forelocks and then pulled forward from her cap just one modest curl, heavily powdered until no black could be seen.

But when it was all done, fear made her uneasy. Suppose Tremblay saw her? If laundering her rankest shift was enough to make him grab at her, would he not pose twice the danger now? She must continue to hobble as if her boil and crooked limbs afflicted her. And if she encountered him while crossing the stable yard, she would find horse droppings to tread in.

"Some solution will come to me," Jeanne whispered. "It always does."

She deceived herself, of course, in believing her improvements were tiny and therefore unlikely to be noticed. What would be the point of making them in the first place, if they truly were? But perhaps she hoped, though unwilling to admit it, that M. Ellsworth would merely grow to mind Marthe *less*. That he would find her *less* repugnant than heretofore, for whatever reason. And that being so, his fondness for the old woman would increase proportionally.

But Charles, already wondering how he could encourage Marthe in matters of clean linens and overall sightliness, noticed at once something was changed.

It was not Marthe's demeanor. She backed into the schoolroom with his breakfast even more timidly than usual and nearly dropped the tray altogether when she turned and saw him already awake and dressed, sitting at his desk.

"Monsieur!"

"Good morning, Marthe." It might have been a trick of the winter light from his now-clean window, or the fact that he was seated and therefore low enough to look *up* at her bowed face, but his lips parted in surprise.

"You are—you are up early," she fumbled, setting the tray on the long table because it was nearest and limping quickly to the fireplace to hunch down.

Charles frowned, bemused, for her rapid movement stirred the air. From habit he held his breath, but when he chided himself and released it—

Lavender? Could that possibly be *lavender* he smelled?

He gave himself a surreptitious pinch. This must be a dream. He was still asleep, and he was dreaming about changes to his chambermaid because it was the last thing he mulled over as he drifted off. He was dreaming she looked ten years younger that morning. That her lank and tortured hair which usually stuck from her cap like denuded stems from a thistle was now coaxed into one smooth ringlet. How old *was* Marthe, when one came to think of it? If she was Bertrand's aunt—and he must be in his upper forties—was she sixty? Seventy?

But if it was all a dream, Charles did not succeed in

waking himself. "If I am up early," he replied, "it is because I was eager to speak with you."

"With *me*?"

"Yes, on a particular matter. How—different—you look this morning! You must have slept well."

She swallowed audibly and managed to nod. "Yes. Thank you."

"Did you know, Marthe, the boys and I were not the only ones at the theatre yesterday? For we saw in the pit your nephew, the footman Bertrand."

Shrinking further into herself, she continued to sweep the ashes. "Truly? Well. Bertrand enjoys the theatre. I hope it was a good play."

"It was two plays. And yes, they were entertaining." To set her more at ease, he removed to Pierre and Georges' table to start on his breakfast.

"And the boys?" Jeanne temporized. She felt even more conscious, to have him behind her where she could not peek at him. "Did they enjoy themselves?"

"Yes. At least, they paid attention, although the action puzzled them at times. I think they would have preferred something with battle scenes or a sword fight." He grinned at the slice of pineapple on his plate and wondered if Babeau had any notion what hothouse delicacies were being diverted to the tutor's morning meal. "But what I wanted to say, Marthe, was that not only was Bertrand there, but he brought a young lady with him who I learned is your great-niece. A Miss Martineau."

To this his chambermaid responded only with a grunt, though she began to scrape the hearth noisily with the shovel.

"Did you hear me, Marthe?" he asked. "Hold off on the fire for a moment. I said your great-niece Miss Martineau was with him, and during the interval I had the honor of being introduced to her."

"Honor?" grunted Jeanne. "She is merely a servant girl."

"Oh. Well—it's always an honor to meet a respectable young lady, and she was certainly that. And I say I was introduced to her, but it so happens we had already met! Before I ever came here, and completely by chance—on the Pont Royal." He waited for Marthe to ply him with questions about the incident, but instead she heaved a log onto the fire dogs and fussed over getting it where she wanted it.

Charles shook his head, rather amused. He had hoped Marthe would be eager and proud to speak of her beautiful great-niece, but this was turning out to be rather uphill work.

"Are you and Miss Martineau very close?" he ventured again, feeling his color rise.

His was not the only heart thumping faster. What would be the best answer to questions like this? Jeanne wondered. Whatever she said, she must remember to tell Bertrand, that he might say the same things. "She is my sister's granddaughter."

"Ah, so she too is from St. Omer?"

"Er...yes?"

He chuckled. "You sound uncertain."

"That is, my sister married and removed to Clair-marais," Jeanne improvised, deciding on the spot to give Miss Martineau her cousin Alice's history. "Very near St. Omer. A farming village."

Charles blinked in surprise. "Indeed? But she told me when I first met her that her father studied in England—like your own. Do you remember in the gardens, when I said you were the second person I'd met in Paris whose father studied there? Miss Martineau was the first! She told me that day on the Pont Royal. Is that how your sister met her husband? He knew your own father from their mutual study?"

Jeanne nearly groaned aloud. In choosing Alice's family story, she had forgotten *again* what M. Ellsworth already knew. How on earth to keep track of all these English-speaking and English-studying fathers of daughters? If she could hardly keep it straight, Bertrand would certainly blunder at some point.

"I do not remember," she lied, feeling her palms break out. "Yes, maybe that was it."

He smiled at her bowed head. "I declare, it makes me feel quite kindly toward all you Collets and Martineaux, to discover your ties to England, despite our countries' frequent conflicts." Marthe made no answer to this, and Charles belatedly remembered her saying that the memory of her father's death was still painful. Safer to keep to Miss Martineau, then.

"So, if Miss Martineau's father was a scholar, did her mother later marry a farmer, or was there only the one man, and he was just a very learned farmer?"

Jeanne shut her eyes briefly. She would have to borrow a slate soon, to record all these lies! "No—Alice's—that is—Jeanne's scholar father died. And her mother as well—my sister, I mean. So the farmer is her stepfather."

"Poor girl, if she has lost both parents. Is that why she has come to Paris to work as a servant?"

"No, monsieur," she said, picking up the thread of Alice's life again. "The problem is there are *too many* Martineaux living. Too many mouths to feed. Therefore Jeanne must work. And that is why," she added in a fit of inspiration, "I too have come to work. My sister's family could not take me in."

"I see. That is too bad." And it was. Charles could guess how this Clairmarais farmer might balk at taking in his dead mother-in-law's sister, if he found even the step-daughter too much to support. But what would become of poor Marthe in the end? There would come a day when she could no longer work, and then what? A shabby room in a boarding house until her savings were spent? Followed by what—the hospital? The workhouse?

"Marthe," Charles said with concern, "if your sister's family could not afford to take you in, I hope you are saving your wages. And you should do all you can to foster your relationships with your nephew and great-niece, for the sake of your future. It is a hard thing to be alone in the world."

"*Merci,* monsieur." She was nearly inaudible. Jeanne had a wild thought she might weep into the ash bucket at these continued proofs of his gentle character or else laugh uncontrollably at the bungle she had made of it all. "I—save as much as I can."

"Good. And what of your relations with Bertrand and Miss Martineau? Can more be done there?"

Panic rising again, Jeanne was curt. "What do you mean?"

"I mean, it never hurts to be in favor with others," he began awkwardly. "That is—Marthe—I hope you will receive this advice in the manner intended." When she made no response, he ran a finger under his neckcloth and forged on. "I, for one, find your company quite pleasant. You are thoughtful and helpful and—forbearing."

At this it was impossible to suppress a sigh. What young woman of twenty with beautiful curling black hair could thrill to such bland, grandmotherly praise? One would have to be an angel to do so. And Jeanne was no angel.

The temptation to fish was too great. Turning just enough to peep sidelong at him, she yielded to it.

"Monsieur," she said slowly, "do you ask me to 'foster' my relationship with my great-niece because *you* would like to foster a relationship with her?"

He shifted in Pierre's chair. "I—er—of course Miss Martineau is—very beautiful. And not only beautiful. She has courage and spirit as well. For—as I mentioned a minute ago—I met Miss Martineau before I came to work here. At the time, she had a bundle of your things, which a thief tried to take, but which we—recovered." He broke off, a line appearing between his brows. Miss Martineau could not be entirely averse to her great-aunt's company, if she had been carrying her belongings that day. How had they met? And where? They would have had to meet twice, in fact—once for Miss Martineau to receive the bundle and once to return it. But why would Marthe have given Miss Martineau such a bundle in the first place? Not to be laundered, that was plain. Nor had it been a purchase Miss Martineau made for her elderly relative, for who gave such stinking gifts?

Jeanne was so delighted by his words she failed to observe his puzzlement. *This was an improvement*, she thought. Beauty, courage and spirit! A smile spread across her face, and she threw him the most fleeting of glances. "Ah, monsieur, how good of you to help her and to remember her."

The line between his brows deepened. "Do you see her often?" he asked.

"What? No," coughed Jeanne. "Hardly ever. No."

"But she will occasionally go upon errands for you, or you for her?"

The perspiration threatening her brow had nothing to do with the fire she had just lit, but she backed away from the hearth nonetheless. Please heaven may her grey paste not run!

"Rarely," she bit out, creeping sideward to take hold of his breakfast tray. "Very, very rarely. I had better return this."

"But I'm not quite finished—"

She grunted in acknowledgement, keeping her hunched back to him and sidling away to his bedchamber. She knew from experience that whenever she had his chamber pot in hand, M. Ellsworth would look anywhere but at her, and she needed this safety now.

Sure enough, the charm of the chamber pot held, and she was allowed to escape with it, clutching it to her stomach like a talisman to fend off further questions. If only she knew as effective a cure for the way his presence and warmth threw her into confusion!

When his maid was gone, Charles pensively made himself a second cup of tea, hoping it would clear his mind. He must have slept more poorly than he thought. Because he had failed in both his goals, having persuaded Marthe neither to any self-improvement, nor to ingratiate herself with her great-niece. And the little information he gained of Miss Martineau, wrung from her unwilling relative, only led to more questions.

But perhaps most disturbing of all—

Setting down his refilled cup, he pushed back Pierre's chair and rose to lean over the fire Marthe had built. He rested one elbow on the mantel, and with his other hand he took up the poker and idly jabbed the burning log.

Perhaps most disturbing of all, Marthe's trace of lavender lingered, and what Charles saw in his mind's eye was not the lovely Miss Martineau, but rather the flash of radiance from Marthe's face when she threw him a smile, a radiance which could not be wholly ascribed to the unexpected glimpse of a full set of little white teeth.

CHAPTER 9

I kept constant to this story, not knowing any better way to
conceal my self.
— John Chardin, *The travels of Sir John Chardin into Persia
and the East-Indies* (1686)

"Bertrand!" Marthe hissed as he passed in the grand
courtyard. She was half-hidden in the shadows
behind the sheds. "I must speak with you."

"Later," he replied. "Raulin has summoned me."

"To serve at Tremblay's dinner?"

"Who knows?" But he suddenly halted and retraced his
steps. "*Ciel!* What has happened to you?" His noble nostrils
flared as he sniffed deeply, even as she retreated. Then, in
what Jeanne recognized as his Mithridate-ordering-
Monime-to-take-poison attitude, he stabbed a finger at
her. "We will talk about this. Oh, heaven, we will talk about
this! I will find you shortly."

Tremblay and various guests were indeed dining,

served by a full complement of footmen, but when Bertrand caught Raulin's eye, the steward raised a brow and jerked his chin toward the adjoining library. It might be another hour before the meal ended, but woe betide Bertrand if he was not found there when he was wanted.

Still fretting over the changes in Jeanne, he thought he might use the time wisely. If he beckoned her from the window overlooking the stable yard, the foolish girl could unburden herself while he took her to task.

But Bertrand was not the sole occupant of the library. He was not five steps into the room before Tonette, of all people, scrambled up from the desk, hastily wiping her currant eyes.

"What is it?" she demanded. "Am I wanted?"

Stopping short, Bertrand held up his hands. "Not by me. Please. Do not let me disturb you. I await the master's bidding. But I am sorry to see you are...distressed."

"I am fine," she said quickly. Too quickly. Tonette then drew a long breath before giving a toss of her chin. "That is, I honor you for the sentiment. It is something indeed, your sympathy. You, with so much already on your mind."

Wary, he raised one lofty brow. "What would I have on my mind?"

"I meant old Marthe, of course," she answered. "And now I hear you have also a niece. No, no, do not look surprised. Of course Madame told her maid Solange and Solange told everyone else."

"The niece is not my charge, in any case," said Bertrand gruffly.

"Hm." She made a wry face. "If you say so. Though you may change your mind after Tremblay talks to you."

It was undignified, but Bertrand gulped. "What do you know, if I may ask?"

Tonette hesitated, cocking her head to listen to the unabated conversation and clink of glass and cutlery from the dining room. Then she came lightly closer, the cloudy winter light from the window falling across her face. Bertrand could see she had indeed been weeping.

"Come," she said. "You can tell me. This 'niece' you were seen with. She is your mistress, is she not?"

"She is not!" He cut the air with a decisive hand. "She is like a daughter to me. A niece like a daughter," he added belatedly.

At the word "daughter," Tonette turned her head away, and when she spoke again, her voice was thick before she cleared it. "Well, if the master wants to have your niece-like-a-daughter, what do you plan to do about it?"

"I must—I will prevent it, if I can," he replied.

He knew Tonette's history, of course. And the fact that he knew—that everyone at the Hôtel de Tremblay knew—was excuse enough for her touchiness and her mask of mockery. Though her seduction by Tremblay and the birth of her child took place before Bertrand and Jeanne came to work in the household, she made no attempt to deny the gossip. Indeed, despite her unfortunate past, with her sharp tongue and reputed riches, Tonette enjoyed more respect and fear among the servants than the less esteemed thought she deserved.

"But how will you prevent it?" she pressed, her eyes whipping back to him and narrowing in challenge. "I do wish I had your confidence, if not your methods."

"Why would you need either?" he asked lightly. But he could not help retreating a step. Ridiculous that she could intimidate him, with her mean stature and snub nose. Or was it his own uneasy conscience?

Tonette's lips parted, and for a moment Bertrand

thought she might reveal the workings of her mind, but then her mouth snapped shut. "I have nothing to lose to him any longer," she shrugged. "I was merely curious. You have not spent all your years here, as everyone else has, so you seem...different. That is all."

With this enigmatic speech, she straightened and, smoothing her fichu, marched from the room.

BERTRAND HAD little time to mull over Tonette's quirks, however. There came the sound of chairs being moved and people in motion, and he had only time to dart to the window at peek about for Jeanne before the door opened and Tremblay entered, followed by Tollemer.

The master ignored him for some minutes, going to his desk and consulting his secretary on various pieces of business and correspondence while Bertrand stared at the wall opposite as if he were carved from stone. But then Tollemer was dismissed and the door shut behind him.

Tremblay rose and paced the room twice, ending at the fireplace, where he placed a nonchalant hand against the sculpted mantelpiece.

"How did you enjoy the theatre, Botlan?"

"Well, sir. Thank you," answered Bertrand, still staring straight ahead.

"I am happy I pay such wages to my servants that they may comport themselves as their betters."

"Sir."

"Do you go often, Bertolan?"

"No, monsieur," he said cautiously. "But I worked many years in provincial theatre, so it is a treat for me."

"And such a fine young lady I saw you with! You quite

put me to shame, you know, for I had only my withered mother for company."

"Mme Tremblay is a fine lady," said Bertrand, for lack of anything better. Improvisation had never been his forte. Indeed, in the old days, if anyone skipped a line or missed a cue, he would be lost for a long minute afterward, and it would require dexterity by other cast members to lead him back into the scene.

"Bah!" Tremblay dismissed the dowager with a wave. "*T'occupe pas d'elle.* Never mind her. Never mind any of the women in my household! I never saw such a collection of ugliness and disfigurement in all Paris. Look, you—I sent the tutor whats-his-name to greet you, and he tells me this girl is your niece. Here is my request: bring her here to work. She may have whatever position she likes, even lady's maid to Madame—surely she cannot make my mother look any worse than she does."

"My—my niece is already employed," dithered Bertrand.

"What do I care for that? What are her wages? I will give her double."

Bertrand felt perspiration prickle. *Bon sang de bonsoir!* Good heavens, what was he to say to all this?

"She is—very satisfied where she is, but we thank you, monsieur."

"Nonsense. She is a fool if she turns down double wages."

"She—loves the family she works for," Bertrand floundered. "I will—try to persuade her—whenever I see her again, but I think it will be hopeless."

"Whenever you see her again!" echoed Tremblay, his color rising. "We need not wait for that. You might send a note this afternoon. Where is this beloved family, and what is their name?"

"I—believe they live in the Marais."

"You 'believe'?" Tremblay banged a fist on the mantel, causing the ormolu clock to jump. "And their name, Blanc-mange? Do not make me repeat myself."

"H-H-Horloge," blurted Bertrand.

"*Clock*? Their name is *Clock*?"

"Or Hortense. Or Nuage. I'm afraid I cannot recall."

Tremblay glared at him. "Whatever their name, you will write your niece at once—or better yet, go yourself to her and tell her of my offer. In the meantime, I will have Tollemer investigate this ridiculous 'Clock' or 'Flower' or 'Cloud' family from the Marais. And if I find you have not been truthful with me..."

Bertrand stumbled from the library, escaping through the door which led to the back staircase. *Quel disastre!* He must find Jeanne at once. This was all, all her fault for insisting on attending the theatre!

He stopped to swab his brow. The dinner hour being ended, there was no telling where Jeanne might be now, and Bertrand had just resigned himself to climbing the many stairs to her cold and cobwebbed attic when he met Louise the chambermaid descending, carrying a basket of laundry. As Tremblay's current favorite, Louise was smartly dressed in canary-yellow taffeta and silk stockings, and Bertrand could not help but think how ill she would take it when she heard the master had his eye on a new maid to supplant her. There would be no convincing Louise that he had nothing to do with it—that he was not trying to bring his family up in the master's estimation. Nor would it help matters any, from Louise's point of view, to learn Bertrand's "niece" disdained the offer.

There was nothing wrong with the servants' gossip network, for Louise said at once, "What did the master want with you?"

A new wave of perspiration threatened him, but he would later be proud of himself, for he managed to strike the pose of Agamemnon defying Achille in *Iphigénie*. "How can you trouble me now?" he thundered. "Do you not see I am unwell? Where is my aunt Marthe? She must help me."

Being no Achille, Louise drew back in alarm from this untoward display. She dreaded all illnesses, lest they be smallpox and mar her plump, smooth face. "What is this? Dimier said your aunt was unwell herself and crept out to visit the apothecary. Faugh! First her stink and deformity, and now she spreads this contagion to you? You keep your distance."

Bertrand gladly obeyed, nodding to her and slipping down the passage behind the carriage sheds. Jeanne was no more sick than he was, and he wagered he knew where to find her.

THE ABBAYE AUX Bois occupied the corner where the rue de la Chaise intersected the rue de Sèvres, just behind the garden walls of the Hôtel de Tremblay, and Bertrand knew Jeanne would often wander past because she liked to hear the light, laughing voices of the girls who boarded at the convent. But there was no sign of her lingering by the gate, nor along either street. Grumbling to himself, he turned down the rue de Grenelle, and it was then he saw her drifting toward him—or toward the Hôtel de Tremblay—and the dratted girl was absently forgetting to hobble!

"Marthe!" Bertrand called. "Dear *old* aunt Marthe!"

She heard him with a startle as if roused from a daydream. But at least she remembered herself enough to crouch lower and affect a limp.

"What is wrong with you?" he hissed, when he reached her. "Where have you been? I thought you wanted to speak with me. And now I must speak with *you*. But not here. Come—we must be out of sight of the house because Louise thinks I am gone to the apothecary and Tremblay thinks—" He stopped abruptly, his nose working again. "I was right, earlier! You do smell of lavender! What is this?"

"Oh, Bertrand, don't scold me," pleaded Jeanne. "I couldn't bear to stink another day, not even a little bit. Not after the theatre. You see, I'm still ugly, but—"

But he had spun her around, to take a hard look at her. "But not as ugly as you used to be. Not as ugly as you *should* be! Listen to me, 'Marthe'—" Taking her arm, he led her away along the rue des Saints Pères where they might not be seen.

"Yes, I will listen, Bertrand," she interrupted, "but first, what would you think of a walk in the Tuileries with M. Ellsworth and me—the real me? Just one short little afternoon's walk?"

"No!" he snapped. "*Absolument pas!* I should never even have agreed to the theatre."

"But you have to," she wheedled, "for I have bought blue silk to make a becoming new hood."

"No," he repeated. "We have done enough damage and have already brought disaster on both of us." Tersely, he told her of Tremblay's demands.

Jeanne's eyes did widen as he expected, but then, instead of bursting into tears or cursing the fates or vowing repentance, she grew thoughtful. Thoughtful as they crossed rue Jacob. Thoughtful as they reached the quay des Theatres.

Bertrand felt his anxiety sharpen. He would have welcomed a tear or two in response. An apology would not have been amiss. At least she was listening, was she not? And if she was listening, she must be thinking of a solution. She must surely be coming to her senses.

"See there, Bertrand?" she said at last, pointing at the Pont Royal.

"Yes, yes, my dear. We have come far enough. Now tell me what we will do."

"That is where I first met M. Ellsworth."

"Confound Ezzwort!" cried Bertrand furiously. "What do you propose we do, Jeanne? I would be surprised if Tremblay did not ask me at supper for my niece's answer, so if we are ever to show our faces there again, we must come up with a plan."

She clutched his sleeve and turned brimming eyes on him. "I know."

"Don't cry," he softened, drawing out a handkerchief. "Your paste will run."

"Yes." She dabbed her eyes carefully, steadying herself. "Yes, you are right. I am being silly. But this evening will not be a problem. You told Louise you felt unwell, and she believed you. Now you have only to return and go to bed in the dormitory. If Tremblay asks or sends someone to ask, you will say you tried to see me, but they told you I was ill. Since you are ill yourself, this will not be strange."

True, true," he agreed, relieved. He smiled to think how clever he had been to put Louise off thus. "That will work, Jeanne."

"For now," she sighed. "And you could plant in his imagination that I was a sickly babe, which would make it reasonable later if she were to suffer illness after illness. But this time around could be the grippe because that takes at least a week to overcome. Who knows? It might not be necessary to invent additional ailments afterward, if Tremblay forgets about her."

"That is trusting a great deal to luck. Suppose he does not forget, or that he ceases to believe me? My niece cannot be sick forever. What then?"

Her bosom rose and fell with another sigh, and she absently rubbed her side where the strap holding her hump chafed her. "Isn't it obvious, Bertrand? If we come to such a pass, we may have no choice eventually but for you to receive the dreadful news that your niece Miss Martineau has died."

"Died?" gasped Bertrand. "But we spoke of killing off Marthe, not Jeanne!"

"What would we gain by killing Marthe?" asked Jeanne sorrowfully. "I must have somewhere to live and work until Easter. And Jeanne can never, never work for Tremblay, or she will be ruined. So, if it comes to that, Marthe must live, and Jeanne must perish. It is that simple—at least as far as anyone in Tremblay's household is concerned because we cannot risk them learning our secret."

He frowned, nodding. "It is fortunate, then, I have much experience playing victims of Tragic Fate."

"Indeed." Jeanne was sorry he made no objections whatever to her suggestion, and she added with a touch of asperity, "But if I might die in a few weeks, Bertrand—or if Jeanne might, rather—won't you *please* let her walk with M. Ellsworth in the Tuileries this Sunday, with you as a chaperon? It may only be possible this once or possibly twice. Please, Bertrand!"

"*Twice*?" he inhaled. "Never! My dear girl, you cannot

make a habit of this! No. Even once is too dangerous. Ezzwort may not tell anyone if he sees Jeanne Martineau alive and well on Sunday, but suppose another servant does?"

"No other servant knows Jeanne!"

"But they know Ezzwort. If they see Ezzwort and me walking with some young woman, they will ask him who she is. We cannot expect him to lie as well."

Her voice thickened with unshed tears. "He would lie if we asked him. If he knew what was at stake."

From what she knew of M. Ellsworth's character, she knew it to be true, but still she held her breath. At last Bertrand gave in. "Very well, Jeanne. But once, and once only. This shall be Miss Martineau's possible swan song, as it were. It will have to be arranged later in the week, however, or how can it be that she is too sick to be seen and can then go for a walk?"

But Jeanne was giving a delighted hop, too happy to get her way to fuss over Miss Martineau's fictitious illness. "She will get better! But we will not tell M. Ellsworth until Saturday. He will understand why you do not want Tremblay to know."

"Oh, Jeanne," he sighed again. "I have a bad feeling about this."

"Oh, Bertrand," she imitated him teasingly, "I have a *good* feeling about this." Cheerfully she took his arm again and swung it. "Come now, we had better go to the apothecary before you take to your bed. We will buy you some harmless medicine, I will spread my magical grey paste on you, and *voilà! Pauvre,* sickly Bertrand."

CHAPTER 10

I went down into the garden of nuts to see the fruits of the
valley, and to see whether the vine flourished,
and the pomegranates budded.
— Song of Solomon 6:11, *The Authorized Version* (1611)

Yves the gardener stumped out from the glasshouse
to accost Charles as he was walking the gardens and
thinking over the next day's lessons.

"I have some *grenades mûres*," he said without
preamble. "I told Marthe to come tomorrow, and you may
come too and bring the boys."

"*Grenades?*" repeated Charles, nonplussed. Did the old
man collect weaponry? Pierre and Georges would be highly
interested, no doubt, but he could not imagine Marthe
wanting to lob one. "What does that mean, *grenades*?"

The old man frowned at him as if he'd lost his wits.
Then he made a cup with his palms. "*Grenade. Un fruit plein
de graines rouges.*"

"A fruit full of red seeds," translated Charles. He whooped with laughter. "A pomegranate, perhaps? You must pardon me. I am still learning. Yes, we would love to come. I warrant the boys have likely never seen nor eaten one. We would be delighted. Thank you, Yves."

With a grunt Yves touched his cap and was gone, shaking his head over the crazy Englishman, while Charles continued his stroll, hands clasped thoughtfully behind his back.

It would be good to have Marthe's company again. For whatever reason, he had not seen her much that week. She tended his room, as ever—the flowers were there, his fire was built, his breakfast was served and removed, his chamber pot emptied—but these things happened either when he was asleep or when Pierre and Georges were present. Nor had she returned to sit through the boys' lessons or to eat her dinner in quiet and warmth. Charles had heard talk in the *office* at the lower servants' table that Bertrand was ailing, so perhaps his aunt was occupied with tending him.

To his amazement, this realization brought a twinge of jealousy. *But I am Marthe's special charge!* No sooner did the selfish, asinine thought flit through his head, however, than he upbraided himself for it.

Ridiculous. Of course she would rather nurse her nephew than listen to him conjugate English verbs or teach the boys to calculate sums.

But still, he found he missed her. She was, after all, the only adult at the Hôtel de Tremblay who troubled herself to speak to him beyond bare greetings. And she was, of course, the great-aunt of the fascinating Miss Martineau. But more than these things, for such a sad, unfortunate creature, she was so thoughtful and kind. There were the little treats added to his breakfast tray. There was the mirror he now consulted every morning when he shaved or tied his neck-cloth or adjusted his wig—a mirror so fine, with its gilt frame and unspotted surface, that Charles feared she might have stolen it from Tremblay's own apartment. In unoccupied moments he played a mental game, imagining poor Marthe in her youth, when her complexion and hair matched the lingering beauties of her hands and her laugh and her smile. It was idle, he knew. Whatever aesthetic heights she might once have scaled—and somehow she always ended in resembling her great-niece—there had always, always been her unlucky deformity.

THE BOYS CHEERED with excitement when Charles announced the day's plans.

"Are my lessons so bad?" he teased in English, and Pierre replied carefully in the same, "They are not bad, but new is good."

It was a grey, cold day with a mizzling rain falling, which made it all the more pleasant to enter the warmth and dryness of the greenhouse. Yves and Marthe stood at the far end beside a large potted pomegranate tree, from which fruits dangled like enormous earrings.

"Come," beckoned Yves to the boys. "I will tell you about this tree and later show you what is inside the fruit." The gruff old gardener took his lesson very seriously, but enough memory of his own boyhood remained that he had prepared tasks for them. Soon Pierre and Georges were in heaven, trimming their own little branches with Yves' assistance and stripping them of leaves, before planting the cuttings in fresh pots of soil.

129

"Marthe, I am sorry to hear your nephew Bertrand has been unwell," Charles murmured at one point as they looked on. He would have appreciated a clear view of her, to determine if he had imagined her improved looks days earlier, but Marthe seemed equally determined to evade this scrutiny. Only the faintest trace of lavender imparted from her hunched figure told him it had not all been a dream.

"Yes," she told the glasshouse floor. "But he improves. It was the theatre outing, I fear. My great-niece fell ill as well, Bertrand says."

"Not Miss Martineau! Dear me. I hope she has someone to nurse her as faithfully as you have Bertrand."

"Mm."

Jeanne thought about the hours she spent—not keeping vigil over the perfectly healthy Bertrand but rather in her drafty garret, sewing her new blue *caleche* and removing a portion of stuffing from her hump. When she had put on the diminished result that morning, panic seized her. Too much! She had removed too much! As a result she hunched lower than ever and promised herself she would replace half the subtracted material that very night.

But first things first. If the walk in the Tuileries was to happen, she must set things in motion. "Jeanne is young," she reminded him. "I am not anxious for her. And Bertrand improves hourly," she said.

"If he does, he has you to thank for it," rejoined Charles, with a playful poke. "Do you add to his invalid's gruel bits of pineapple and orange and Babeau's best, as you do to my breakfasts?"

He could hear the smile in her voice when she replied, "There is nothing special in your breakfast."

"I see. It is a point of pride then, for M. Tremblay, that his servants dine like princes. At breakfast, at least. For I must say, neither at dinner or supper in the *office* do I find such tasty little flourishes."

"Bah," said Jeanne. But still trying not to chuckle, she stole a peek at him and was disconcerted to find his blue gaze fixed on her. At once she regarded the tile floor of the glasshouse again, though her heart gave a flip like a fish on a line, and she felt heat flood her cheeks. Ah, but the man was dangerous!

"There it is," Charles murmured, half to himself.

"What, sir?" mumbled Jeanne.

"Your smile," he answered thoughtfully. "A young lady's smile. I noticed it the other day. And not only because you still have all your lovely teeth."

"I take care of my teeth," she blurted, her hands clutching each other. "Because they are my one vanity."

"Wait—but you told me your youthful hands were your one vanity."

"No—it's my teeth. Certainly my teeth. I don't know what you're talking about."

He laughed softly. "I won't begrudge you more than one vanity, Marthe. I told you before you may have two, if you like. For that matter, you may have ten."

"Never mind an old hunchback like me," she insisted. "You would do better to mind your teaching, instead of foisting it on poor Yves."

"In my defense, Yves appears to be having a grand time," Charles answered. "I'm curious, however—is it Yves who lets you take what you like from his toil here, or do you filch the goodies from Babeau?" Reaching for her sleeve, he gave it a mischievous tug. "With these graceful hands of yours?"

Jeanne's breath caught. If Marthe had been a young woman, a straight and smooth one, she would have imagined M. Ellsworth was flirting with her. But with Marthe as she was—why, even with her trifling improvements, no one but possibly the odious Tremblay could overlook her repugnant *tout ensemble*! Therefore, this could be no more than M. Ellsworth's friendly disposition.

Whatever it was, it was too much for Jeanne's tender heart, and she turned with a scoff. "*Quelle bêtises!*" she scolded. What nonsense. Retreating to the potting table, she took up the little knife there and set to work slicing the oranges Yves had set out.

"Ah, yes," said the gardener, straightening. "Come, Pierre, Georges. Marthe will demonstrate the proper way to cut open a pomegranate, as I taught her. Show them, Marthe. I have this bowl here for the seeds."

Obediently she began to run the little knife around the calyx end of the fruit while the boys gathered to watch, their eyes just above the level of the table. Georges even absently leaned against her, and without meaning to, Jeanne threw Charles a startled glance. One corner of his finely-cut mouth tipped upward, and he shrugged as if to say, *You see? I am not the only one who suspects you of hidden charms.*

The revelation of the pomegranate's abundant seeds in their juicy, ruby-colored arils brought sighs of pleasure from the boys, and when she tapped the seeds gently into the bowl, Pierre and Georges eagerly accepted Yves' invitation to try them.

"We will have a little feast," he declared. "You see our industrious Marthe cut you some oranges as well. Pomegranates and oranges are a match fit for a king. Come, I insist. Everyone must try everything. There are many more fruits to come, and the master will not even notice the lack."

Not that anyone required much urging. At this time of winter, fresh fruit was a delight. M. Ellsworth praised the flavor, while his pupils expressed their agreement by eating a great many seeds and finishing the orange altogether.

It was after Marthe sliced a second orange that disaster struck.

She had refrained from eating any of the first one so that the boys might have their fill, but by the second she neatly trimmed the rind from a slice and popped it in her mouth, just as Pierre cried, "*Regardez!* Look!" He opened his mouth wide to reveal the segment of rind placed precisely over his teeth, a uniform orange grin.

Jeanne choked with laughter. They all did, but Jeanne choked literally. She felt the chunk of fruit in her mouth fly to block her windpipe. *Ciel!* Her hand clutched for her throat, her eyes wide with panic, but as everyone was still looking at Pierre, it was only the boy who noticed.

At once he sprang to her side, stretching up to give her as powerful a thump on the back as he could muster. His little fist caught her squarely in her hump, accomplishing absolutely nothing except to make him recoil in shock, piping, "*Dégueulasse!* Disgusting! It's spongy!"

Fortunately and unfortunately for Jeanne, M. Ellsworth understood the crisis in an instant, and undistracted by Pierre's revulsion, he thrust the boy aside. Winding his arm up, he gave Jeanne's back an almighty blow, which succeeded in dislodging both the orange chunk and her hump itself. The orange chunk flew across the table to land in an empty pot, while her hump swung nearly up to her shoulder, perching unnaturally one endless moment before she regained sense enough to coax it down with artful writhes and contortions.

All was hubbub. Yves and Georges crowded close, questioning and exclaiming, and Pierre burst into tears for proving so unsteadfast a rescuer. Still panting, Jeanne tried to alleviate the former's concern while comforting the latter, but all the while she was acutely conscious of M. Ellsworth's silence and furrowed brow. She was acutely conscious that he was puzzling in his mind over what his hand had encountered. No bony protrusion, as both Pierre and he expected, but rather the much softer yielding—the *sponginess* of stuffing.

"I must get back to work," Jeanne croaked, when a measure of calm was restored.

"Yes, yes," said Yves, "and you had better have a cup of coffee or wine to soothe your throat. I must work as well. Good-bye, children, M. Ezzwort."

Jeanne hastened away as fast as she could hobble, pretending she did not hear M. Ellsworth call, "May I speak with you later, Marthe, to ensure you suffered no harm?"

Let him think her deaf now. It hardly mattered. She must find Bertrand at once, or the game would be up!

CHARLES HAD every intention of interrogating his mysterious chambermaid on this newest discovery, but when he did not catch her the following day, he determined to rise before dawn on Saturday to waylay her. It was not Marthe who came to deliver his breakfast and lay his fire that morning, however. Instead he heard a heavy tread, and the door opened to reveal a solid woman with a disconcerting long hair sprouting from a mole on her chin. She gasped at his unexpected appearance, nearly dropping the tray she carried.

"Pardon me, sir," she muttered to the handsome young man at his desk. Marthe had made no mention of the tutor rising with the owls, and Dimier hastened to set his breakfast on the nearest surface.

"Good morning," he returned. "But where is Marthe?"

Though Marthe had prepared the laundress for the question, everything flew out of Dimier's head with those intent blue eyes upon her. "I don't know," she managed.

One eyebrow arched in skepticism, but Dimier put her head down, plowing ahead to the fireplace, where she proceeded to bang and scrape and clank to such a degree that Charles understood she did not mean to be disturbed in her work.

Very well. But he would not be thwarted so easily. When the lessons were done for the day, his next thought was to accost Bertrand at dinner. But the footman reportedly still kept to his bed, and thus Charles made his first visit to the *chambres des domestiques*, the servants' dormitory which comprised one wing of the second story.

His knock provoked a great rustling and thumping before the command to enter was given in a suitably weak voice. Bertrand lay in bed with a cloth over his eyes, of which he lifted a corner to peep at his visitor.

"Ah, Ezzwort," the footman said, his voice restored to its usual strength. He tossed off the cloth and pulled himself to a sitting position, scratching at his unwigged head. His nightshirt looked suspiciously like a *shirt* shirt. "Shut the door behind you. I was going to send for you myself, soon."

Surprised, Charles complied before taking the chair

Bertrand offered him. "Thank you, Bertrand. I congratulate you on your recovery."

"Yes."

Charles nodded at a little vase of flowers on the bedside table. "I see your aunt has been taking good care of you, as I suspected. It is actually of Marthe I came to speak."

"Marthe?" echoed Bertrand. "Whyever would you want to speak of Marthe? Heh, heh. Good old Marthe. But you had better hear my news first, monsieur."

Smothering his impatience, Charles acquiesced with a polite nod.

"It is my niece Miss Martineau!" announced Bertrand. "I do not know if Marthe told you, but she also caught this accursed cold. We are better now, thankfully, and to celebrate, she and I propose to walk in the Tuileries Gardens tomorrow. With you, sir, if you will accompany us."

"Walk with Miss Martineau tomorrow?" It was perhaps the only subject Bertrand could have brought up to distract Charles from his burning curiosity. "Why—yes. Thank you," he replied. "I would be delighted to come with you. Though Miss Martineau told me at the theatre that such an activity would be burdensome to you..."

"Today it sounds like paradise," returned Bertrand, with a flick of his fingers. "I am not made for lying in bed. To a man of active mind, ennui causes as much suffering as any malady. When would be convenient for you, Ezzwort? I will send Jeanne a note."

"As soon as ever you like," Charles answered. "I awake early."

"A little before ten o'clock, say? You and I could set out then and be there by a quarter after."

"Perfect." Charles hesitated, remembering Miss

Martineau's reluctance to invite her great-aunt along, as well as his own determination to promote a closer relationship between them. With his assistance, Miss Martineau would surely come to appreciate Marthe's sterling qualities.

Having thus persuaded himself, Charles added, "What would you say to inviting Marthe, Bertrand? Miss Martineau said such an outing would be too arduous for her great-aunt, but Marthe may rest on one of the benches if she grows tired. I think it would be as much a treat for her to go as for any of us."

Bertrand could not reply straight off, for some obstruction of the throat occupied him a minute with hemming and hawing. "No," he barked at last. "It won't do. Marthe hates walking. Her back, you know."

Charles looked at him sharply. "Yes. Her back. Now that you mention it, that reminds me, Bertrand. If I may ask, what precisely is the problem with Marthe's back?"

"How should I know?" Bertrand tossed back. "She is my aunt. One does not ask one's aunt about such things. It has always been there. Her hump."

It would have been polite to drop the matter, Charles knew, but he could not. Not when he had felt and seen what he had felt and seen.

To the older man's surprise, Charles rose from the chair to sit on the edge of Bertrand's bed.

"You must pardon me," he said in a lowered voice, over the man's sputtering. "If I may ask, have you seen Marthe today?"

"Er—yes. Briefly."

"Then perhaps she might have told you that, while she was in the glasshouse with Yves and the boys and me, she choked on a piece of fruit." He paused, observing that

Bertrand now mopped his forehead with the cloth he had used to cover his eyes.

"She told me little Pierre and you came to her aid," Bertrand conceded. "So quick and valiant of you, Ezzwort."

Charles shrugged off this praise, too intent even to acknowledge it. "Bertrand, I must tell you: when I thumped Marthe on the back to dislodge what was choking her, I felt that her hump was not bone or indeed anything solid. It was...soft, like a cushion. And it...gave...when I struck it. It moved. As if it were, indeed, merely a pillow fastened to her."

Bertrand shut his eyes. The moment was upon them. Jeanne had indeed come straight to see him, to tell him of the morning's alarming development, and the two of them had argued at length in undertones. Bertrand had been for outright denial and for Jeanne's immediate construction of a new hump with tighter straps and something bony and solid within, but Jeanne had insisted M. Ellsworth would not be fooled. "He is no idiot," she had protested. "He will never believe I grew overnight something permanent and bone-like where there was merely something soft and moveable the day before."

Jeanne won, of course, but Bertrand had still held out hope that shyness or courtesy might prevent M. Ezzwort from raising the subject if Bertrand tried to steer him away. No such luck.

Bertrand took a slow breath, and then threw back his head, gazing into the distance in the attitude Jeanne would have recognized as his Sertorius Recognizing He Might Never Return to Rome. "Ezzwort," he began solemnly, "you must be aware of the lurking dangers of the Hôtel de Tremblay."

When Charles did not respond immediately, Bertrand

raised a finger to silence the words which had not yet come. "I will speak further only on condition of utmost confidence. You may repeat nothing I say, or I will *say* nothing."

His heart speeding, Charles assured him of his discretion, offering that same *parole* Tremblay had scorned.

Bertrand nodded. "Very well. Marthe believes you can be trusted, and I myself trust her judgment. Therefore I will speak." Dropping his Sertorius pose, he leaned closer, so that his voice was barely audible. "You know the master's fondness for...troubling the women of the household."

"I do."

"It is not safe for any woman to work and live here, no matter her age or appearance, if she would resent such attentions. And—Marthe—my aunt—has always been virtuous. Even if she had not been deformed," Bertrand added quickly.

"But that is precisely what I must know," rejoined Charles, trying to match the older man's whisper, despite his own impatience. "Bertrand, *is* your aunt deformed, or is her disfigurement a ruse?"

Another mop of the cloth across Bertrand's brow. This was the plunge.

"Yes," he admitted. "It is a ruse. You must tell no one, monsieur. Not a soul. The hump is for her protection."

"I understand," said Charles, placing a hand to his breast. "I tell you again, I would do nothing, say nothing, which might endanger poor Marthe."

Bertrand's answering smile was genuine. Jeanne was right: the Englishman was a good lad. There was no possible path for Jeanne and Ezzwort to be together, but he was a worthy young man. He hoped Ezzwort would be satisfied and take himself off at this point, and Charles did rise, but at the door he stopped again.

"If Marthe does not, in fact, suffer from her back, are you certain she would not like to join us tomorrow morning?"

"Positive," replied Bertrand roundly. With finality he lay back again and slapped his cloth over his eyes. "She is still, after all, old as the hills."

CHAPTER 11

You still wrangle with her, Boyet,
and she strikes at the brow.
— Shakespeare, *Love's Labour's Lost,* VI.i.1100 (1597)

"Jeanne replied to me that she will meet us at the east end of the Terrasse du bord-de-l'eau," Bertrand told Charles on Sunday morning. It being his holiday, the footman had put aside his livery with its telltale gold braid, and Charles might have mistaken him for a lord, so handsomely was he clothed in brown broadcloth and damask.

Charles too had taken particular care in dressing. He wished Marthe had come, that he might consult her, but it was Dimier again who shambled up the stairs.

"Is Marthe unwell?" he asked the laundress. "Did she catch what Bertrand had earlier?"

"Eh? What is that? I cannot understand you—your accent. Impossible," complained Dimier, though she had understood him well enough the day before. Therefore he had only his mirror to advise him, and it told him his eyes gleamed with excitement and his color came and went.

It was a lovely February day. A frost covered the ordure of the streets and lent sparkle to the city, and they strode quickly to warm themselves.

When they passed through the entrance along the quay and turned to walk the long tree-lined terrace with its river view, Charles at once picked out Miss Martineau in her blue wool dress and cloak, approaching with her light step. On this occasion Mme Tremblay could have found no fault with her coiffure, as her curls were dressed high and well powdered, protected by a becoming blue caleche.

"Miss Martineau, what a pleasure," Charles said as he made his bow, aware of the rapidity of his pulse. "I am very glad you are well again."

"Monsieur," she curtseyed, favoring him with a demure smile. "*Et mon oncle.*" This to Bertrand, who kissed her on either cheek.

"M. Ellsworth, do you mind if we speak French, so my uncle will understand?" asked Miss Martineau.

"Of course," Charles assured her, even as Bertrand grumbled, "I have no need to listen to sentimental nonsense. Talk all the English you please. I will sit on the first empty bench."

"But then you will not be chaperoning us," she observed.

"Bah! If you keep to the Grand Allée, Ezzwort is such a great tall fellow, I will see if he takes advantage of you, even if you are halfway to Place de Louis XV."

The two young people needed no further persuasion, Jeanne gladly taking Charles' arm. Admiring looks followed the pair, and he thought he would burst with pride.

"Tell me about this family you work for in the Marais," he began in French. "Have you been there long? Do you like them?"

"I will tell you nothing," she rejoined in English, but her face dimpled. "Because both times I have seen you, you have asked me this and that, and I have never learned anything of you. Perhaps you have some horrible secret you want to keep hidden. I should know this because, if it is bad enough, I will not want to walk with you."

Jeanne was indeed curious to learn more about him, but she was equally determined to avoid spinning further complicated tales about herself if she could help it.

To her surprise, he sighed. "Miss Martineau, you already know the worst of it. I told you at the theatre of my debt and how I came to be a tutor in Tremblay's household."

"If that was the worst of it, I have heard worse, I dare-say." (Nay, Jeanne was certain she had recently *told* worse!) "Come. I know your recent misfortunes, but you must begin with where you are from and your people. Were you, in England, a very *grand seigneur*? You were raised perhaps on a large estate with a thousand servants at your beck?"

"Not a bit of it," he replied. "I hope you will not be too disappointed, Miss Martineau. My father is a gentleman, the son of a clergyman in Winchester who had the good fortune to hold a relatively prosperous living. He wanted my older brother William to become a clergyman too, but once William took his degree at Oxford, he said he would not do it, and that I had better be the parson of the family."

Her eyes widened. "And does that please you? Will you like to be a parson?"

His smile was deprecating. "My father said I should take this trip to decide. If William was going to live as a gentleman of leisure, my father wanted me to have my travels and adventures too, before I settled to sermons and ceremonies."

"And you *have* had adventures," she prompted. "Have you not? Did you go to Italy before you came to Paris?"

Charles hesitated, and they watched a quartet of *grisettes*, bold and laughing, emerge from the chestnut trees of a side alley. Shop assistants and seamstresses, they cast critical and envious looks at the girl and her companion.

"Here is where I will lose more of your good opinion," he resumed thoughtfully. "For I intended to go to Italy from here, and possibly as far as Austria, but now it will never be. Because there is no more money for it. You see—William— and I have gambled it all away."

She cocked her head at him. "It was gambling, then, in your case? Not the purchase of too many paintings and sculptures and personal finery?" (This given with a playful tug on the lace spilling from his cuffs.) "Ah, then M. Ellsworth, you are too hard on yourself. Many of my countrymen are hardened gamblers. Unless you were such yourself, or unless you refused to play altogether, I do not think you could have avoided your difficulties."

After his long self-recrimination, her sympathy was a balm.

"Does your brother also work to recoup his losses?"

Charles thought of William's airy letter. Whatever he was doing now, it likely did not involve much exertion. But his smile was fond, if rueful. "I suspect, if William manages to improve our family fortunes, it will be through his charm, rather than his labors. He is remarkably handsome."

"Yes," teased Jeanne, laughing. "I am so sad you are the ugly brother."

Instead of joining in her joke, a shadow fell over his

countenance. "Just so. I—know beauty is important to you," he said. "You being so lovely yourself."

Jeanne flushed at his compliment, even as unease prickled, and she halted in their progress. "M. Ellsworth, if you mean to praise me, why do you also sound as if you were finding fault?"

"Not finding fault," he rejoined quickly. "I am sorry it sounded so. No. It is simply that—well—I wonder if I might say a word in favor of your great-aunt."

"Of *Marthe*? That is, my great-aunt Marthe?" Taking his arm, she pulled him into motion again. "Shame on you, monsieur, if you think of my poor great-aunt when someone mentions ugliness!"

It was his turn to color and stop. "You're right to chide me. I confess I did think of her because I know—the world—would call her ugly. I do not do so myself. Not any longer, if I am to be honest. I am too fond of her now."

"*Vraiment?*" her voice was barely audible as she lapsed into her native tongue. Truly? "You are fond of her?"

"Very much so. In fact, I do not know if you know, but she choked on some food yesterday—do not be afraid, she is unharmed—but afterward I felt such a pang when I thought of harm coming to her. She has been so kind to me."

"You are fond of her like—a mother?" asked Jeanne.

He considered. "I don't actually know. My mother died when I was quite young."

"Like a governess or a nursemaid, then," she suggested. "I am certain she must be...fond of you in the same manner."

Charles thought of Pierre and Georges' maid Fournel. Did Marthe feel toward him as Fournel did toward her charges, a mixture of exasperation, fatigue, and affection? Heavens, he hoped not!

"She...cares for me," he tried to explain. "But more like a friend and...fairy godmother. Do you know the term?"

"I know." Jeanne hid a smile. Why, it was perfect and delightful. She was his good fairy? Even ancient and wrinkled and hunched, he thought of her so? With an effort she fought down the urge to throw her arms around him and hug him tightly. M. Ellsworth might never see Miss Martineau again, unless she could somehow convince Bertrand otherwise, but Miss Martineau would see M. Ellsworth every day hereafter in the person of his dear Marthe.

She raised glowing eyes, and Charles contended with his own desire to crush her in his arms. He glanced down the *allée* to where their chaperon sat on a bench, his head not even turned their direction. He could do it. He could kiss her. But what would it mean? At home in England it would mean they were engaged. But here, where he had no money to live on, much less to support another—here, where even his time for the next year was not his own— here it would be meaningless. It would be amusement. Or seduction.

It was not the thought of Bertrand which stayed his impulse.

It was Marthe.

He could not repay his one friend and fairy godmother by dallying with her young relation. By promising what he could not fulfill.

Shaking his head to dispel his troubling thoughts, he gave her a jocular nudge. "You know what I would like to do, Miss Martineau?"

"Tell me." A tiny sigh of disappointment escaped her.

He had wanted to kiss her—she knew it. Did he refrain because they were in public? There were so many hundreds walking in the gardens that morning that not a soul would have noticed. They would not even have been the only ones, for among the milling pedestrians were couples holding hands, faces close together, sharing a peck or a longer embrace.

"I would like to take you and your great-aunt Marthe out together," he declared, as if announcing a great treat. "Don't you think she would like the Café Renard on the riverside terrace?"

Again Jeanne halted, releasing his arm, lest he discover the tension suddenly stiffening her. "Oh! What a—pleasant idea. But I have told you already—she would not be able to walk so far comfortably."

"Suppose I were to hire her a sedan chair?"

"No." Jeanne held up a peremptory hand. "You are penniless, and with the bouncing and swaying of the chair she would be seized by *mal de mer*."

To her alarm, his jaw tightened. "In the first place, Miss Martineau, I may not have the funds to discharge my debt to Tremblay or to spend the next six months in Italy and Austria, but I nevertheless have a few *sous* for a sedan chair and three cups of chocolate. And in the second place, do you know for a fact Marthe would suffer nausea, or do you have another reason for not wanting her to come?"

She blanched. Did he *know*? Could he possibly have guessed? "What other reason could I have?" The words emerged more harshly than she intended.

"I wish you would tell me," he said, holding up his palms. "I would like to see you again, and clearly Bertrand only accompanied us today out of generosity. Marthe would be a welcome chaperone in his place, and if she derived enjoyment from an outing, why, that would make me even happier."

Her breath returned to her body.

"Miss Martineau, I should tell you, if your uncle has not already, that I learned her—hump—is...not real. Not a genuine affliction, that is. I wonder if some of her other physical weaknesses might not also be assumed."

"She is old," cried Marthe desperately. "It is true she adopted her hump for protection, but she is very, very old. Old and weak and-and-and it would be cruel of you to make her do what is neither easy nor pleasant merely so you are not inconvenienced."

"Inconvenienced?" echoed Charles, astounded. "I beg your pardon. I confess I thought such a proposal might please you as well. Would you not like to meet again next Sunday?"

"I have to go to mass."

"We might go together, if you like. And walk afterward."

"After mass I am never in the mood for frivolity."

"Oh. Well—before mass, then."

"We might—" Jeanne steeled herself "—we might walk by ourselves. With no chaperon." It was a gamble. M. Ellsworth had only to turn his head and look around and he would recognize how many couples of their—that is, of *her* —class were unchaperoned.

His face grew stony. "Miss Martineau, this will sound prudish to you, I imagine, but in my country it is not at all the thing for a young lady to walk alone with a young man."

Jeanne felt her own face flame in response. Before she had become an actress and before she lost her parents, she would never have made such a suggestion either. Nor would she have made it now, to any other person but M.

Ellsworth, who was so plainly, so obviously a gentleman. A girl could not be safer than with him.

Seeing her discomfiture, his sternness melted. "Please, Miss Martineau. Won't you tell me why you had rather Marthe not join us? I understand she is neither...fashionable nor...pretty, but—"

"My great-aunt Marthe dislikes me," blurted Jeanne. "Because—before I became a chambermaid, I was on the stage, and she disapproved."

Having convinced himself Miss Martineau's reluctance sprang from embarrassment over her not-always-presentable great-aunt, this revelation took him aback. "You acted on the stage? The public stage?"

"I did." Her chin lifted defiantly. "I take it you share her disapproval, M. Ellsworth. In your country is it 'not at all the thing' for a young lady to appear as an actress on the public stage?"

He released a slow breath, struggling to be fair. "To be frank, it is not. Not for daughters of gentlemen, at least. I cast no aspersions on your character, Miss Martineau, I merely speak what I find to be the case. Is it not the same in France?"

"It is the same," she admitted after a pause. There was Eglantine, after all. And Olivier's Pauline. Both actresses and neither one particularly concerned with the proprieties. If she felt anger at M. Ellsworth, it was the anger of knowing she could not deny he had cause for suspicion.

"How came you to be in service, then?" he wondered.

Jeanne almost smiled at her freedom to tell the truth, for once. "Our little troupe's managing director stole our receipts and many of our accoutrements. I had no choice but to find other work."

149

"Does...your uncle Bertrand know you worked as an actress?"

She laughed merrily. "Oh, M. Ellsworth, Bertrand has been an actor too. We were in the same troupe."

"Then does Marthe disapprove of him as well?"

"My uncle Bertrand is a man," was her simple reply.

They had begun to walk again, reaching the great octagonal pool, but Jeanne's hands were in the pockets of her cloak and Charles' clasped behind his back.

"My honesty has cost your good opinion," she murmured, when they stood before Coustou's sculpture of Summer.

He frowned over this, too aware that some part of him *was* disappointed to deny it, but soon his natural modesty reasserted itself. Who was he to sit in judgment on her? He, who had recklessly endangered his own claim to gentility? And he had less excuse than she. A girl forced to earn her bread must do *something*, but he—he had nearly lost everything because he hoped to cut a dash among the fashionable in Paris!

"Miss Martineau, forgive me taking a minute to accustom myself to the idea. I am surprised, yes, but of course you have not lost my good opinion, if you consider it worth having." He gave a disarming grin. "But have pity on a poor clergyman's grandson who has never met an actress and knows of them only as mistresses of princes and noblemen."

"They are the mistresses of mayors as well," Jeanne conceded, returning his grin. "But not *this* one." She lay a hand to her breast and dropped a curtsey.

He bowed in return. "No one who meets you would question your respectability, Miss Martineau, and if your great-aunt Marthe does, well, you leave that to me."

"What do you mean?"

"I mean that, to show my good faith, I intend to broker a peace between you. I have so few friends in France that I cannot have two of them avoiding each other."

Ciel! Jeanne groaned inwardly. Why was this M. Ellsworth so everlastingly determined to bring the two halves of her together? Now either she or Marthe must be cast as the villain. *Unless we kill off Miss Martineau,* a little voice in her head reminded her. But she smothered the thought as soon as she had it. Not yet! Oh, please, not yet.

Because each time she saw him she grew greedier.

First she must have the theatre. Now this walk in the Tuileries. And next—oh, please, might there be just one more time? He might kiss her, if she could have but one more time.

IT WAS NOT TO BE.

For at that moment, a disorderly group of older boys nearly collided with them, too intent on the leather ball they were hurling back and forth to watch where they were going. One knocked into Jeanne and received sharp words, whilst the ball whistled past, nearly taking Charles' wig with it. Being both taller and quicker, he leapt to intercept it on its next flight, drawing cries of protest.

"*Allez jouer ailleurs,*" he commanded. Go do this somewhere else! And to encourage them in obedience, Charles reared back to fling their ball as far as he could, only to have the two largest youths seize his arms and wrestle him down.

Jeanne shrieked as the rest of the gang joined the tussle. Beating the nearest backs with her fists, she saw the ball roll out from the scuffle and snatched it up. Running some distance away, she shouted, "You want your ball? Go and fetch it!" Then, with a throw that would have won Charles' admiration, had he not been buried under three bodies and unable to witness it, she slung it with all her might. The little orb hurtled in the direction of the nearer horseshoe ramp and would certainly have reached it, if only Jeanne's accuracy matched her strength. As it was, an obstacle interrupted the ball's flight.

An obstacle in the shape of a man's head.

Fortunately it was the back of his head, but the blow was sufficient to remove both his hat and his wig. His female companion screamed, and the victim of this outrage let loose a cry and an oath. Then he straightened and, with frightening leisure, step by measured step, turned to face his assailant.

Horror flooded Jeanne, and she began to babble apologies before her hand flew to cover her mouth. Because she recognized the injured party. Taking a quiet step backward and pretending to inspect the statue of *Renomée,* she might yet have escaped detection except the man's companion had keen eyes.

"*Tiens*, Hubert!" cried the older woman, frightening in her thick paint and swaying coiffure. "How familiar that girl looks, does she not? Like the footman's niece from the theatre. Same blue dress beneath that cloak, same face. But I thought he told you she was ill."

Not that Jeanne stayed to hear Mme Tremblay's musings. Heedless of Tremblay's calls and trusting M. Ellsworth to take care of himself, she escaped into the strolling throng.

CHAPTER 12

Resolv'd on this, she gently Death bespoke;
Take heed you do not mis-direct your Stroke.
— Edmund Arwaker, *Truth in Fiction* (1708)

"You say they saw you?" Bertrand demanded, appalled. "Both saw you and recognized you?"

The two of them were hurrying across the Pont Royal, Jeanne having hardly dared to explain herself. She had not even paused beside his bench in the garden, but rather darted by, panting, "Bertrand, come at once! We must go."

"I am certain of it." Breathlessly she recapitulated the scene at the western entrance and saw him go a greeny-grey. "Oh, Bertrand! I am so sorry. What rotten luck."

"It's more than that, Jeanne. It's catastrophe! Tremblay will summon me the moment he arrives home, and I do not doubt he will accuse me of lying and dismiss me at once."

"You—could say you did not know I was recovered."

"Bah! He will ask why I did not send word for you the instant I myself was on my feet again."

Tears filled her eyes, but she dashed them away, thinking furiously. "Perhaps we could say—we could say you *did* send word. That we were walking together in the Tuileries, and you told me I must come to work at the Hôtel de Tremblay, and I refused, and you were angry with me, and I ran away from you. Yes! That could work."

"That could work for one day," Bertrand retorted, "and then, when you do not come tomorrow, *then* he will dismiss me. And I do not suppose he will keep Marthe on, if he has ejected her nephew. No, *ma chère*, we will both be turned out to grass. And where will we find another position for a mere two months? They accepted us here because they knew me, but another place—" He fluttered his fingers expressively.

They turned into the rue de Sorbonne because the Tremblays would surely return by the rue du Bac.

Jeanne's jaw was mulish. "We *cannot* go to another place, Bertrand! Even if we neglected to tell another household we would only be there until Easter. Because if we go to another place, I cannot see M. Ellsworth every day."

"Ezzwort?" bellowed Bertrand. "We face starvation in the streets, and you are only concerned with whether or not you see this Ezzwort every day? Ah, *que les jeunes sont stupides!*"

"Young people aren't foolish," Jeanne protested, as he nudged her toward the rue des Saints-Pères. "It is that you have grown too old to remember love."

Halting abruptly, he tapped an insistent finger on her forehead, like a woodpecker hammering at particularly thick bark. "Listen to me closely, Jeanne. There are but two possibilities now. One: I tell Tremblay your story of what happened in the park; he says, Very well, send for her tomorrow; I say, she will not come; he says, then you and your old aunt must go."

"And what is the second possibility?" she whispered.

"Two: I tell Tremblay your story of what happened in the park; he says, Very well, send for her tomorrow; I pretend to obey, but then I receive the heartbreaking reply that—*helas!*—Jeanne Martineau is dead. I beat my breast. We don mourning. The crisis is averted."

"But how would I die so suddenly, when Tremblay saw me perfectly well minutes ago?"

He frowned, considering. "You must be run down by a carriage or—crushed by a wine barrel or—or fall down the stairs and break your neck."

"Perhaps I could choke on something."

"Of course you could not choke on something!" argued Bertrand. "Not when Marthe just choked on something."

"But Marthe survived," Jeanne pointed out, adding dreamily, "because of M. Ellsworth's valor and quick thinking. Besides, if Jeanne were to choke to death so soon after Marthe nearly did, it would be rather poetic."

"Poetic—bah! It would be suspect. *Non! Absolument non.*"

"Jeanne could fall from the Pont Neuf, then, and drown. Or from the top of Notre Dame."

"Someone would have to push her from the Pont Neuf," insisted Bertrand, "and what would she be doing on the top of Notre Dame? No. Those would look like suicide. It had better be a carriage running her down."

Jeanne sighed. "Oh, Bertrand. If it must be. I suppose I was crossing the street and forgot to look? What a—what a commonplace way to die."

"Commonplace is precisely what we want. Nothing

suspicious about it."

They had reached the corner of rue S. Guillaume and by common instinct withdrew into the tiny alley to finish their planning.

"You must give the performance of a lifetime, Bertrand," Jeanne commanded him, when they had worked out the probable eventualities and consequences.

"I understand." He threw off her admonishing hand, the better to strike his attitudes. "When Tremblay calls me in, I tell of how I tried to persuade you, only to have you dash away. I am angry! Such disrespect to her uncle's wishes!"

"Yes," agreed Jeanne, adopting their master's supercilious and dissolute expression. "And what do you propose to do now, sirrah, if you intend to keep your position?"

Bertrand shrunk and bowed. "I will insist, monsieur. I will go to the Marais myself and drag the girl out."

"You had better! Because Tollemer found no Clock family or Flower family or Cloud family residing in the Marais—"

"Forgive me, monsieur. They have some foreign name I can never remember that *sounds* like a French word but is not. But I will go to this home and insist my niece return with me."

"You will go at once!" thundered Jeanne, pointing as if to a door.

"At once, monsieur." Bertrand straightened then, letting the act fall away. "Then I will return later, weeping and carrying a bundle of your things, to announce your death."

Jeanne nodded, drooping at the thought of handing over her blue dress and new caleche, as well as a petticoat, most likely, and her oldest shoes and stockings. Tremblay would confiscate these pieces of evidence, she was certain, and then would she have to see Louise or Barbe flitting about in them?

"Word will travel like lightning," she resumed, "which is why I will take care to be in the schoolroom with M. Ellsworth, if I can. We would not want him to hear it from anyone but you, and you must come as soon as you can after telling Tremblay. Remember, Bertrand—the performance of a lifetime!"

He placed a hand to his breast. "One worthy of the *Comédie Française* itself. You had better look to your own performance, rather than fret over mine, for I have been on the stage as many years as you have been alive."

IN THE FLURRY of her unplanned departure, Jeanne had no time to think how M. Ellsworth experienced the matter, but when Marthe climbed the steps with his breakfast the following morning, she was not entirely surprised to find him dressed and standing by his window.

"Again so early," she murmured.

"Good morning, Marthe. I hoped to catch you."

She nodded, pressing her lips together so no smile of bittersweet joy escaped her. Jeanne Martineau might never see M. Ellsworth again, but Marthe could and would.

It was better than nothing.

It would have to be.

Setting his tray down on his desk, she carried the little vase of flowers to the side table next to him. "Here I am, then," she addressed his waistcoat. It was raining again, and she was grateful for the faintness of the light falling on her. "Did you...have a nice walk with Bertrand and Jeanne?"

"It ended rather suddenly," he replied. When she turned toward the fireplace, his hand shot out to grasp her sleeve, only to release her instantly when he felt her shiver. "Forgive me, Marthe, for startling you. I simply wondered... have you spoken to Bertrand since he returned from the walk?"

"What? A word or two in passing. Why?"

"That is good to hear. Because—you see—yesterday your niece and I were enjoying our pleasant stroll down the *Grand Allée*, when we were involved in a little scuffle with some boys playing ball. I ended up on the ground for a minute, and when I managed to throw the youths off, I discovered she had gone. I looked all around and retraced my steps to where we left Bertrand sitting on a bench, and he too was gone, and I have not been able to find him here. Did he not mention it to you?"

"Not a word," lied Jeanne stoutly.

"Then, we do not know if he escorted Miss Martineau home, or what became of her?"

"Oh, Jeanne." She waved an airy hand. "Bertrand would have said something if he was concerned. But he and I know Jeanne can take care of herself."

"I am glad to hear it and certainly hope it was the case, but it was odd that she did not say good-bye."

Jeanne gulped. Clearing her throat, she hobbled to the fireplace. Considering Jeanne Martineau would be giving up the ghost in the course of the day, what harm would a black mark on her character be? She had only to say, "Ah, my great-niece is so flighty and inconsiderate. I am not surprised, sir." But the words would not come.

But, as if Jeanne had indeed spoken, M. Ellsworth said, "Marthe—she told me of her past work on the stage and of how you did not approve of it."

"Oh? Well, who cares for an old woman's opinion?" retorted Jeanne, taking up her little broom.

"I think *she* cares, Marthe. And certainly I value your good opinion. It pains me to think there might be any... coolness between family members and people I care for."

"I do not say she was being thoughtless when she disappeared," Jeanne rejoined, softened. "She is a good girl."

"Yes," he said, his voice lifting. "I think so."

She began to sweep the ashes into the pan. "Perhaps my great-niece felt suddenly ill again. Or she—needed the privy. Too embarrassing to mention to a young man, you know. I hope you will forgive her for running off like that. As I said, she is a good girl, and I know she...liked you."

"You know she 'liked' me?" he asked eagerly, striding to crouch beside her. "You mean she told you? Or her uncle? Or what do you mean she 'liked' me? *Passé?* Does she no longer?"

"Likes," Jeanne amended, annoyed with herself. "*Likes* you. *Au présent.* She—er—told Bertrand after the theatre, and he told me."

A wide, honest smile lit his features, and he laughed, sitting down on the floor now and reaching for the dish from his breakfast tray. "Marthe, I could kiss you for telling me so. In fact, I *will* kiss you for it." Tossing down the pastry he had just picked up, and before she could comprehend his meaning, the tutor leaned to grasp her by the shoulders.

Jeanne gave a panicked squeak, and then his lips were on her cheek, planting a long, hearty smack. He released her, still chuckling, but when his eyes met her wide dark ones, his mirth died in his throat.

"Good heavens. It's not done, is it?" he breathed. "I've

done something unforgiveable. I thought you French were always kissing—"

"No—it is not unforgiveable," Jeanne muttered, her blood still rushing in her ears. "It was...very kind. But—my face is dirty." Whipping a handkerchief from her sleeve, she scrubbed the grey paste from his lips with grandmotherly violence and then stuffed the cloth back in her bosom before he could see the telltale smears.

Then he was laughing again, his fingers touching his mouth. "Mercy—are they still there? I thought you were going to scour my lips clean off."

She pretended not to hear him, instead crawling halfway into the hearth to arrange the wood and kindling, while furtively rubbing her cheek to repair the damage. Ah, if she had been alone, it would have been a different story. She would have sat for an hour, clasping her knees and reliving the moment, and she would not have touched her cheek except tenderly, imagining his kiss again!

He withdrew to his desk to eat, now whistling cheerfully, and when her heart was restored to its usual rhythm, Jeanne spared a pang to think how soon his good mood would be dashed.

THE MOMENT CAME JUST before M. Ellsworth was set to dismiss Pierre and Georges to dinner. Jeanne sat in the back of the schoolroom, mending M. Ellsworth's shirt and stockings, as she had most of the morning, waiting and waiting for Bertrand's step on the staircase.

"Bertrand!" exclaimed M. Ellsworth warmly. "How glad I am to see you. You may go, boys. Pierre, don't forget to clean your slate, and Georges, thank you for putting the books away." When they had obeyed and vanished to thump and shout their way down the stairs, M. Ellsworth turned on the footman with alacrity. "Please do tell me what happened yesterday. I could find neither you nor Miss Martineau, and I was just sharing my concern with Marthe."

Bertrand cast a glance at his conspirator, who continued to sew quietly, but she pulled the thread so taut it snapped. *Performance of a lifetime*, he told himself.

"Monsieur Ezzwort, I have just come from speaking with M. Tremblay," he began, his voice slow and solemn.

"Oh?" The tutor did not quite succeed in hiding his impatience over both the non sequitur and the older man's pace of speech.

"I say this because M. Tremblay sent me to call on my niece this morning. M. Ellsworth, you remember our earlier conversation about the master's interest in women of all sorts?"

"I do," answered Charles warily. "As well as his interest in Miss Martineau when he saw her at the theatre."

"Exactly," intoned Bertrand. "A man from whom even such as my aunt Marthe is not safe without a false hump—"

Here a gasp from Jeanne interrupted them, and Bertrand lost some of his gravity. "Oh—then M. Ellsworth has not even mentioned to you that he knows? Sir, I congratulate you on your discretion."

Charles gave a brusque nod. As much as Marthe's false hump had interested him two days earlier, today it was merely a delay in him learning what he wanted to know. "Please, Bertrand, go on. I take it Tremblay's designs have extended to your young niece?"

"Yes, that is it. He wanted me to send for her days ago, but I told him she was unwell. But then they happened to see each other in the Tuileries garden yesterday. Jeanne fled, and this very morning the master told me there was no more excuse: I must fetch my niece or both Marthe and I would be dismissed."

"What are you saying?" demanded Charles roughly. "You cannot have delivered Miss Martineau to that man's clutches!"

"No, monsieur! Marthe and I would beg in the streets before we did such a thing."

"Then, what?" Charles stared from one to the other. Now that he knew Miss Martineau to be safe, a stab of distress caught him off guard. Then Marthe was going? Had she already known of the possibility that morning?

She folded her sewing and laid it aside, rising. "Your cuff is mended, sir."

"Confound my cuff!" he swore. "Are you going, Marthe?"

"We are, are we not, nephew?" she consulted Bertrand, the tremble in her voice having nothing to do with acting a part.

But however convincing Jeanne's performance was, Bertrand's equaled it, and she was aware of an amused respect for his abilities. For here he put a hand to his brow, and when he spoke, he out-trembled her. "There is no longer any need, aunt."

"What do you mean?" cried his two auditors simultaneously.

"I mean," he choked, "I mean I went myself to the home in the Marais where Jeanne works. Worked. I went to tell her she must leave her comfortable position and seek another, as must Marthe and I, but that we would combine our savings. But—but—"

"But what?" pressed Jeanne and Charles.

The man's throat worked and an actual tear dropped from his eye. "But I came too late! Our little Jeanne is no more!"

Jeanne screamed and affected to faint, and such was Charles' shock that he did not move a muscle to catch her, leaving her to soften her own landing as well as she might. But no sooner did she tumble noisily to the floor than the tutor remembered himself enough to bend down and ask if she were injured. After she pretended to regain her senses, she gave a shake of her head, and he assisted her to rise before returning his aghast gaze to Bertrand.

"How is she no more?" he asked, hardly audible. "What can you possibly mean?"

Bertrand extracted his own handkerchief and blew his nose, trumpet-like. He had concealed a slice of onion in its folds and emerged more tearful than ever. "They told me...it was at the *quatervois*—the cross-way along Rue des Lombards—so abominably dangerous! My Jeanne—you know with what speed and sprightliness she walks, monsieur—Jeanne came gamboling along, her mind on other things, and the next thing anyone knew—"

Jeanne let loose a sob and flung herself at Bertrand, squeezing him enough to say, *Well done, but what of Tremblay?* And he returned the squeeze reassuringly: *He took me at my word.*

Then she did fight back tears, but they were ones of relief. "Will you take me to see her, Bertrand?"

"Better not," he said, blowing his nose again. "Her injuries—it would give you nightmares."

"Will there be a funeral?" M. Ellsworth's low voice throbbed with emotion, and Jeanne's clutch on Bertrand tightened guiltily. It was both flattering and painful to see how their news moved him.

"Just a quiet little word for Marthe and me with the priest at the Holy Innocents' Cemetery," replied Bertrand, having no desire to go through a sham ceremony with the young man beside them, not to mention the expense of paying someone to play the cleric.

"I understand." Charles sank into Georges' chair, putting his head in his hand. "I did not know her long, of course, but I—please accept my condolences." He swallowed, and Jeanne could not forbear trying to comfort him.

"Ah, monsieur," she murmured. "You are so kind. One day I would have rejoiced to see my great-niece marry someone like you. I mean, if she were not a humble servant girl and actress, and you an English gentleman."

He shook his head, a touch of rueful amusement visible even then. "You are determined to make a King Cophetua of me, Marthe."

"A who?"

"Have you not heard the story of the king who loved the beggar maid? Well. That's the gist of it. But the difference between Miss Martineau and me was, in truth, not a fraction so great. She was—a lovely girl," he concluded inadequately.

A silence fell, as if they played a scene for which an end had not been written. Bertrand raised an eyebrow, pointing at the door with his chin, but Jeanne replied with an infinitesimal shake of her own. No. He might go, but she wanted another minute with M. Ellsworth.

Therefore the footman's groan was genuine. But their plan had worked, and the young Jeanne was safe. If old Marthe chose to make a fool of herself now, well, that was trouble for another day.

CHAPTER 13

And then doo what I can, alas, my Heart beginnes to sturre.
— Nicholas Breton, *The Toyes of an Idle Head* (1577-1582)

The fortnight which followed would be indistinct in Charles' memory. He did his duty as a tutor; he ate; he slept; he answered when spoken to. He counterfeited living, if he did not actually live.

His brother William later showed him a letter Charles wrote at the time, and while there was no mention of his grief, its shadow appeared in the line, "I took a walk to the Cemetery of Holy Innocents today and hate to think of anyone lying there till the last trumpet. It was a jumble of graves enclosed by arcades of the charnel houses, all within hail of the markets. There was no peace there for the living or the dead."

Wherever Miss Martineau was buried, he could not find her grave without assistance, but of course he could not ask Bertrand or Marthe.

Charles told himself it was ridiculous to mourn someone he had only conversed with three times, however delightful and stirring those times had been. However beautiful and vivacious she had been. He might have offered for her at the end of his servitude when he was free of debt, but how would that have fared? He would still have been penniless and she in service, and even if money were found to carry them back to England, who knew if Miss Martineau would have been willing to go? To leave home and country and family for...him.

There was no point in pondering these things now. None at all. But still, he wished he might wear black wool as Bertrand and Marthe did, to mark her loss and his brief but genuine affection for her.

The season of Lent began, but Tremblay secured the necessary dispensations for his household so that, apart from sole and waterfowl being served thrice per week, rather than once, Charles noticed no difference. What he did remark, with a jar, was the maid Louise twirling in the *office* before dinner, showing off the new dress the master bestowed on her. Miss Martineau's blue wool *robe à l'anglaise*.

"M. Tremblay said Bertrand's niece had no further use for it, poor girl," she explained to the other women at the lower table, "so now it is mine."

After one of these meals of sole and Louise's dress, when Charles crossed the stable yard, he noted the sun emerging. The days following Miss Martineau's death had blurred with smoke and rain and darkness, but here, like a friend returned from a long journey, appeared faint warmth and hope. He turned his steps to the garden.

"You will wear a groove in the gravel paths," old Yves

told him some while later. "I will have to rake it level again."

"Your garden is the perfect place to think."

Yves nodded. "But it is cold out, monsieur. The sun has hidden away again. If you would prefer to think in the orangery, I built a new fire in the stove."

CHARLES FOUND he was not the only resident of the Hôtel de Tremblay to seek the cozy privacy of the orangery. He was not there five minutes before the door opened and Tonette stalked in, followed by Tremblay's valet Montaiglon.

"I tell you I have nothing to say to you," snapped the maid, before Charles could rise from the stool between Yves' potted orange trees. "And you are never to lay another hand on me, do you understand?"

"What airs you give yourself, refusing me," Montaiglon snarled. "Who are you but a lowly maid who has lost her reputation? You should be grateful for my attentions."

"What choice did I have with the master?" she lashed at him. "None! What choice did I have, to keep my child? None! But now that my favors are no longer wanted by M. Tremblay, I am at last my own, both my person and my wages."

Montaiglon barked his scorn. "Your wages. Yes, you have saved up your precious dowry, have you not? But who will take you for a wife? I do not see that you have many callers, and the handsome tutor shows no interest in you."

Instead of shrinking at this, Tonette tossed her head. "You think I want to marry anyone within this household or without, much less you? Ha! I have better plans for my money than to give it to some man who will drink it away or spend it on himself. I save not for marriage but for my sister. Sabine will never suffer what I have suffered, if I can help it."

"And supposing I do not intend on being refused?" the valet asked ominously. "It is no easy thing to find a good valet. I am certain the master would prefer to keep me, over a troublesome maid with whom he is no longer infatuated."

"If I must go, I must go," she answered quietly, "but I will take care to inform Tollemer who causes the disruption and inconvenience."

Charles saw Montaiglon blanch, and he remembered the secretary's cool assertion from weeks earlier: "You mean nothing to me, young man, but the smooth running of the household means much." Apparently Charles was not the only servant Tollemer intimidated. With visible effort, the valet rallied to parry this blow, but what emerged was no more than mumbled defiance, and he soon flung from the glasshouse with violence that set the panes rattling.

Tonette released a slow, heavy breath. "Ah, Sabine," she sighed, again opening the door Montaiglon slammed. "What will become of us?"

Having no desire to be caught playing eavesdropper, Charles waited several minutes before rising from his seat. Awkward as it had been, however, he was not sorry for the experience. Tonette's declaration that she cared nothing for anyone but her sister carried the ring of conviction, and Charles was glad no danger awaited him there. But of equal importance, he appreciated the reminder that he was not alone in unhappiness. Every person carried his secret anguish, and his own grief, while real, had turned him inward and blind to those around him.

"I have been selfish," he said quietly, "when I could try to be a comfort to others. At least to Bertrand and Marthe, who knew Miss Martineau far longer and more intimately than I."

As if the heavens approved his recognition, the orangery door opened again, softly this time, to admit the same Marthe he had been thinking of.

She moved slowly, as was her wont, a basket on her arm, and unlike Tonette and Montaiglon, her gaze swept the orangery before she shut the door behind her.

"M. Ellsworth!" It was hardly above a squeak. Marthe lowered herself in a creaky curtsey. "I can return another time, if you would prefer solitude."

"I might say the same, Marthe, unless you would welcome help with your task. Have you come to pick oranges for my breakfast?"

"Yes." She drew closer, raising timid eyes for a glance at him. "You have been...quiet and out of spirits lately, and I wanted to cheer you."

At her kindness, his throat swelled. "Dear Marthe, I should be comforting you. I have lost...a new friend, but you have lost your sister's grandchild. I know that, though you were perhaps not on the best of terms, nothing can supply the loss."

"Not on the best of terms?" she repeated softly. "Oh, it was only that I had hopes of her marrying one day, and while some men would deign to marry a servant, especially one who has saved a substantial dowry, who would marry an actress?"

Charles laid a gentle hand on her shoulder, but whether it was intended to comfort the old woman or himself would have been difficult to determine. "And I have told you, Miss Martineau's beauty and charm were such that...I do not doubt some would have been willing to overlook her... past."

Marthe made a little sound in her throat that might have been approbation or skepticism or merely phlegm, and after a moment she stumped past him to squeeze the oranges nearest her. He reached above her to test the ripeness of the higher fruit before a thought struck him.

"Marthe. I know already that you adopted your 'hump' as a protective maneuver. There was the evidence of my own hands when you choked, and Bertrand and I discussed it later, and I do not blame you for it. But—if I may ask—*is* there anything wrong with your back? You continue to stoop..."

"I must stoop at all times," she whispered. "To inculcate the habit. Imagine the disaster if I were to forget! But, no, monsieur, I will confess to you that there is nothing wrong with my back."

"Apart from any damage done by affecting a stoop all day long," he chuckled, only to break off suddenly, the realization striking him that this was the first time he had laughed in a fortnight. The first time since the morning he kissed her cheek, before Bertrand appeared to deliver his wretched news.

"You're good medicine, Marthe. Come—no one is about—let me see you straighten. If Tremblay pops up from behind one of the pots, you can always don your smelly shift again."

"M. Ellsworth!" But after a hesitation, and with a sound suspiciously like a stifled giggle, she obeyed.

"No, Marthe. Straighten all the way. You are forever keeping your head down. If you are neither hunchbacked nor crooked, you cannot persuade me there is something wrong with your neck."

The hesitation was longer this time, Marthe's beautiful young hands taking hold of her black wool skirts to wring them. But then gradually, almost defiantly, she lifted her head and looked him in the eye.

His lips parted in surprise. Instantly her boldness evaporated, her head drooping again, but of its own accord, his finger shot out to tip her chin upward. "What is—going on here?"

If she could not duck her chin, she could lower her eyelids, and she did, but he could feel the pulse of panic in her.

"Look at me, please, Marthe."

He waited and, after a little eternity, she raised wary eyes.

"You are not crippled in any fashion," he ventured.

"No." She did not say the word so much as mouth it.

"Your walk—your limp?"

A tiny shake of the head.

With a sharp breath he strode away from her, halfway down the length of the glasshouse, where he stopped, beating a hand against his thigh. Then he marched back.

"You must pardon the impertinence of this question, Marthe, but are you even *old*?"

"I—I—" Her bosom rose and fell. Oh! What answer should she make? Suppose she were to reveal herself at once—would he not stagger under the weight of the truth? To find the girl he had been told was dead, very, very alive before him? Would he understand and forgive the deception?

To her horror, tears brimmed in her eyes, and she hastily applied her handkerchief, too aware of the damage they would do to her paste if allowed to run down.

But Charles accused himself of brutality. Good heavens!

Had he not just vowed he would be a comfort to her, and here he went at once, prying into her secrets and protections! And this when she herself was still mourning her great-niece.

"What a clumsy ass I am," he muttered, putting his arms around her and gathering her to him. "I'm sorry, Marthe, for asking you such intimate questions. Please say you forgive me."

But Marthe said nothing of the kind, only erupting against his chest in audible sobs and making Charles feel even more remorseful. "There, there," he soothed helplessly. "How hard things have been. My conduct this morning notwithstanding, I wish you would indeed consider me a friend and confidant."

The words were scarcely spoken before Charles found himself wronging her in a new manner, for however old Marthe was or was not, she did not have the body of an old woman. Or not the body Charles supposed an old woman to have. Beneath the layers of clothing, the one in his arms was lithe and *youthful,* firm where it should be firm and soft where it should be soft, and a treacherous warmth filled him.

"Marthe." It emerged no more than a rasp. He would have put her from him then, but one of her arms had stolen around his neck and one of his was about her waist, and a strange delirium of grief and longing—or perhaps loneliness and longing—or possibly just longing—possessed them. And in this delirium, Charles bent his head, and the woman he held lifted hers, and their lips met.

For a moment outside of time, everything fell away. Their ages, their identities, their circumstances, their surroundings. There was only the warmth of their kiss, the mingling of their breath, the straining to be closer. It could not have lasted long. Only long enough for Charles to cradle her face in his hands as he fought with the last remaining rational part of his brain not to caress her person, and long enough for her to murmur his name. Not "M. Ellsworth," but "Charles."

It was a particularly loud snap from the burning wood in the orangery stove which recalled them. Marthe leapt from his embrace like a deer at the huntsman's gun, burying her face again in her handkerchief and fleeing blindly, nearly falling over the basket she had left on the floor. Before Charles could call after her she was gone, leaving him to slump back to the gardener's stool, mind spinning and blood rushing.

The first conclusion he drew, when sanity began to return, was that Marthe was no more Bertrand's elderly aunt than he was. No aunt of a middle-aged man could make the speedy and agile escape she just had. There was definite relief for Charles in the realization that he had not just kissed within an inch of her life someone old enough to be his grandmother. For, a man who would do such a thing —who would be safe from him? It would be a sure sign that Charles was going the way of Tremblay and soon would be pawing everyone from Dimier in the laundry to Barbe in the scullery.

So whatever age Marthe was, she was much younger than she purported to be. Could she be Bertrand's sister, then? Or another niece? Or even—Charles shuddered—the footman's mistress?

And why had he responded to her the way he did? Even if he was not so abandoned as Tremblay, was there not something wrong with him, that he could spend a fortnight grieving Miss Martineau and then turn right around and accost another woman, even if that woman were not—Lord have mercy—the young lady's great-aunt?

Who was Marthe? How old was Marthe? He flushed, remembering their kiss and only too aware that he would be glad to repeat it. It was not possible to be in love with someone you knew nothing about, of course, Charles admonished himself. Especially if an hour ago thought yourself in love with someone entirely different (of whom you also knew almost nothing). He was a fool. And now what would his poor maid do, if she did not wish to have his attentions forced on her again?

But here even his natural modesty could not prevent him thinking, *I would wager Marthe enjoyed that as much as I did*. But what would she now expect? Seduction? Marriage? Her weary, lined face appeared in his mind's eye, and Charles felt a pang. He refused to ruin her, but if the opportunity offered, could he bring himself to marry her? Could he bring back to England such a bride?

Had she been as young and beautiful as the late Miss Martineau, he would have answered with a resounding yes, Charles admitted to himself with shame. But because Marthe was...older and less attractive, would he then refuse to treat her with the same honor? He imagined returning to Winchester and presenting her to his family and community. Poor Marthe, the humble, worn French chambermaid. To spare themselves disdain and ridicule, would they not hide away from those he knew in his former life? Take some small lodgings a distance from his family, but near enough that Charles could still walk into Winchester to work at something (for he suspected he might be cut off without a shilling, if there turned out to be any remaining shillings of which to deprive him). And would there be children of the union, or would Marthe be past that?

One thing was clear: he should not kiss her again if he did not mean to treat her honorably. He gave a regretful sigh. Really, he should never have kissed her in the first place, but the damage was done, if damage it was. So he must either apologize now and never touch her again, or continue to pursue her, knowing he must then call her his own.

It should have been a simple choice. Ninety-nine men out of a hundred would have dismissed poor Marthe at once from their thoughts, but Charles Ellsworth—he remembered her friendship and generosity, her humor and her difficult circumstances. He remembered her kiss. However old she was, she was not so old that fire did not burn in her veins.

He made his decision then.

If Marthe could accept him, he was hers.

That did make him chuckle. Was he such a prize, that he should hold himself above her? A foolish young man who had squandered his riches, could not call his time his own, and had no idea how or when he might return home, nor if he could ever support a family?

Holding up his palms, he said aloud, "Let it be, then. I will be as good a husband as I am able and suspect I may turn out to enjoy the greater blessing."

He would have risen then to go about his day, but above the glasshouse the clouds parted. An approving sunbeam penetrated the clear panes, bathing him in warmth. And when the beneficent light fell upon his open hands, Charles stared. Frowned.

He held his hands closer, turning them this way and that. He ran a tentative finger over one.

For there on his palms, the same palms which had tenderly clasped Marthe's face, shone distinct smudges. Grey ones. He rubbed his fingertips together, feeling the slight greasiness.

The slight oiliness.

Of paste.

CHAPTER 14

It has brought me into so many confounded rogouries, that
I fear I shall be exposed at last.
— Richard Sheridan, *School for Scandal,* II.ii.23 (1780)

With her face a streaked and smeared disaster, Jeanne had no alternative but to make a beeline for the attic, handkerchief raised as a barrier. With those she encountered, she gave loud sneezes which both explained her hidden face and caused them to veer away with patent disgust. But no one could have guessed what else the handkerchief hid.

Joy.

Joy, pure and utter.

When she reached her ladder, she gave way to the emotion, laughing richly. She took up her skirts and swirled in a circle, round and round the ladder's base, sighing with delight.

Who knew a kiss could be like that?

To this point in her young life she had received only the salutes of family members or friends. The kisses she received on stage did not count: she turned her back to the audience, and Olivier would bend his head toward hers, and they would hold themselves thus for as long as necessary. Not only did space remain between them, but Olivier would frequently use the opportunity to grumble about something which had gone wrong in the scene.

But this—! This wonder! Hot and close, tender and urgent. Breathless, she put her own hands to her cheeks, closing her eyes and remembering his touch.

What would happen now? She could not think. She wanted a moment not to think. A moment just to live and remember and rejoice.

Languorously, Jeanne made her way up the ladder, singing to herself. She pulled off her wilted servant's cap to toss it on her lumpy mattress, only to freeze with arm uplifted, inhaling sharply. For there, beneath the rafters which had never before sheltered anyone but sad old Marthe Collet, stood another.

"Please, don't let me stop you," said Tonette. "Who knew you could sing and dance? Not bad for a woman of your afflictions and advanced years."

"What—are you doing up here?" breathed Jeanne, feeling faint.

"Admiring your privacy," answered the maid. "Raulin stowed you here to spare the rest of us your ripe odor, but you improved in that respect, did you not? Especially since the tutor came."

Her bold eyes raked Jeanne's smeared face and straight figure. "And now I observe other changes, ones affecting even your very person! Your posture, your agility. Have you stumbled upon a fountain of youth, my dear Marthe? Come on, climb up here. I won't bite."

Jeanne was not entirely certain Tonette would *not* bite. At least, not figuratively speaking. But unless the woman meant to expose her immediately, Jeanne must repair the damage to her paste, or everyone in the household would know, Tonette or no Tonette.

Cautiously she crept the remainder of the way up, dispensing with any show of decrepitude. With an enigmatic smile, Tonette made room on the lumpy mattress.

"You have been a clever creature, Marthe," she said. "I would never have known or guessed. But now that I have learned the truth, there is no harm in satisfying my curiosity. Do tell—was the elaborate disguise a means to avoid my fate?"

Jeanne swallowed. But with Tonette's frank currant eyes upon her, she knew the woman would not be put off by polite disavowals. "Yes," she answered.

Instead of appearing angry, the maid nodded, and there was respect in the arch of her eyebrow. "I see. Well done. I applaud you. How did you come by this skill in disguising yourself?"

"I was in the theatre," Jeanne replied quietly. "In the same troupe as Bertrand. I am not his aunt, obviously. But Tonette—what do you mean to do with me?"

"I have not yet decided. But I will make use of this information, you may be sure." She nudged the distraught Jeanne with her foot. "Go on. I suppose you did not come up here simply to sing and dance. You cannot go about looking like that, if you mean to keep others in the dark. Go on. Repair yourself."

Like an automaton, Jeanne lowered herself to the floor, lifting the board to retrieve her items. With Tonette's unblinking gaze on her, she carefully cleaned the ruined paste and charcoal from her face and prepared to apply it anew. But Tonette's hand caught hers.

"Ah, but you are beautiful, Marthe. And young. Very young." She lifted the one lock which trailed from Jeanne's coiffure. "Is this a wig?"

"No."

"Ah. And this, I warrant, is a natural curl—not one obtained with curling-tongs, for how would you manage it?"

In response, Jeanne took hold of Tonette's slippered feet. "Tonette, please! Do not tell anyone. It will not be for much longer—"

"Why will it not be for much longer?"

"Because either Bertrand and I will leave after Easter for another theatre troupe, or—or—"

"Or what?"

But this was a sentence Jeanne could not complete because she herself did not know the alternative. What— would Bertrand go, and she stay on, to be near M. Ellsworth longer? To what end? To be his mistress? As if such a handsome young man would make a mistress of an old woman! He had kissed her, yes, but young men with no one to love might kiss anyone, for a hundred reasons. He was lonely and full of youthful passion; Marthe's little overtures had therefore held out unusual, inexplicable charm, and he had yielded to them.

And would she, who had donned this ridiculous disguise in the first place to protect her virtue, yield to another man—even a better one—if he offered? She *should* not. No, not even if her heart was willing.

But she might. Oh, she might!

Releasing Tonette, Jeanne sat back and pressed a hand

to her breast, as if it could soothe the pain there. No, that was why there was no alternative. Not if she were to remain true to herself.

"—Or nothing," she concluded gruffly. "There is no 'or.' At Easter the theatre troupes sign their new contracts, and Bertrand and I will leave here, never to return."

"*Mais si*," said Tonette, cocking her head. But yes. "There *is* an 'or,' and I suspect it has something to do with our English tutor and the happiness I seem to have frightened out of you. You love him, I suppose."

In response, Jeanne could only bury her face in her hands.

"And he," continued Tonette, "in his native kindness or, more likely, because he is a man and cannot help it, has given you some encouragement."

"He is honorable!" hissed Jeanne, this aspersion of her beloved M. Ellsworth rousing her. She clambered up, prepared to be magnificent in wrath, only to club her head on one of the low attic beams. "*Fils d'âne!*" she cried, gripping her brow. Son of a donkey!

"If he is so honorable," Tonette mused, unmoved by Jeanne's mishap, "then why are you distressed when you think of him?"

Abruptly the maid stood, her own diminutive height protecting her from such accidents as Jeanne had suffered. "Never mind that now, Marthe. If you are determined to be a fool, that is none of my business—at present. There is only one woman's fate which concerns me."

"Your own?" suggested Jeanne bitterly.

Tonette made a wry face. "If that is meant to wound, *chère* Marthe, you have failed miserably. No. I have made a decision, with which you will help me, if you want your secret kept."

"What is it?" Inwardly, Jeanne was already vowing that if Tonette intended any harm to M. Ellsworth or Bertrand, Marthe's secret would have to be exposed, come what may.

But it was nothing like that.

"My sister Sabine is in Paris," announced Tonette. "Where or why is not important, but I want her near me. I came up here to see if I could hide her." She regarded Jeanne measuringly. "Sabine would not have been happy to hole in this tiny, cold garret for any length of time, however, keeping quiet as a mouse. I am glad she will be able to come out and work."

"You would have your sister work for Tremblay?" marveled Jeanne.

"Not for a million *livres*!" Tonette retorted. "But my *brother* can. My *brother* will be safe from Tremblay. That monster attacks any woman who moves, but he seems to leave the boys alone."

Comprehension dawned on Jeanne. "Ah...you intend to disguise Sabine as a boy?"

"No, *idiote!* I intend *you* to disguise Sabine as a boy. With your skills she will become my brother—Armand, say. Armand, who must be banished to live in the attic because he—because he—"

"Because he has fleas?" suggested Jeanne. "I can easily give him flea bites, which of course he must not touch or they will smear, but he could scratch himself elsewhere from time to time."

Tonette flicked her fingers, but her glance at Jeanne showed a new appreciation. "Fleas, yes. Raulin will not assign Armand to the *chambres des domestiques* if he has fleas. The others would be in uproar. But will flea bites be enough to keep them at a distance during the day? It is too bad you used the stinking trick already."

"We could do fleas and then perhaps...a festering sore?" Jeanne pondered. "Or spots? Pimples. I always pity those with *rousseurs*."

"*Les rousseurs,* yes," breathed Tonette. She thrust her hand at Jeanne. "We have a bargain, and I give you points for cleverness, Marthe. I will fetch her immediately. Tell me at once what we will need."

THOUGH CHARLES too had gone in search of Bertrand, it was Tonette who first found the footman, trailing Raulin and several others from Tremblay's office.

"A word, monsieur," Tonette purred, just touching his sleeve. "I think you will want to hear what I have to say. It concerns your so-called aunt."

"*Soi-disant?*" he echoed.

As she expected, he halted abruptly and followed her without another word into the inner court off the *grand cabinet*.

"You are upset," she remarked, "before I have even spoken."

"You will know soon enough," he replied, "when we are all in turmoil. The master throws a grand banquet for the Abbé Teray himself, controller general of finances. Raulin is in a fit. We have not enough staff, nor enough time for all the food to be cooked. Even those not used to it must be pressed into service and livery found, that the master give a good impression."

"Would it not be better to make a poor impression?" asked Tonette derisively. "Or the minister will think the master not only collects the taxes, but also lines his pockets with the country's money."

"Tollemer declares a good impression will imply the collection of the *vingtième* and *capitation* go well," Bertrand answered, referring to the income and poll taxes, "and we are to report by tomorrow morning with our own tax if it is not yet paid."

"Bah! What a nuisance," Tonette grumbled. "I will have everyone from Barbe to Dimier asking me for a loan. But never mind that. Do you not want to hear my news?"

Relating the master's demands had given Bertrand time to stuff down his apprehension at the maid's address, so that he now bowed his head in the manner of a sovereign condescending to hear the petition of a beggar. In spite of herself, Tonette was impressed.

But it did not take long for her story to make an end of his pretended equanimity.

"She admitted to you—" Bertrand gasped, as grey as ever his supposed aunt had been.

"She could not avoid it," said Tonette with a shrug. "But you need not look like that. I can keep my end of the bargain, if you and she can keep yours. If you tell no one 'Armand' is actually Sabine, no one will ever learn from me that Marthe is neither crippled, old, nor ugly."

Bertrand struggled briefly. This development was not welcome; it was not comfortable, but it need not be a catastrophe. At least so he decided. No sooner did he conclude this, however, than she added, "But I would be obliged if you would satisfy one point of curiosity: is she your mistress?"

Bertrand inhaled so sharply he began to choke, and the glare which blazed from him would have incinerated a lesser person than Tonette. "She—is—not!" he strangled. "There has been no one for me since my sainted wife! Jea— Marthe, that is—is like a daughter to me!" At this double blunder, he went from grey to purple, and to their mutual surprise, Tonette put a gentle hand to his arm.

"Peace, peace, Bertrand. There is no call for apoplexy," she soothed. "I already guessed she was young. Perhaps not as young as that, but young in any case. So Marthe is not her real name, then?"

Despairing at his stupidity, Bertrand sank onto a bench and mopped his face with his handkerchief. He could hardly scold Jeanne for carelessness, when he himself crumbled at the first touch! Now the dangerous Tonette held even more weapons in her hand, and it was his fault.

"We will keep our end of the bargain," he promised hoarsely.

He expected the maid to plume herself and toy with him a while, like a cat with a mouse, but she surprised him.

"Tell me..." she murmured, sitting beside him, "why is she like a daughter to you?"

He sighed. "You heard her: we belonged to the same theatre troupe. There is a feeling of camaraderie which develops. No—stronger than that. A feeling of family. We had been together since the previous Easter, you under-stand. We traveled together, worked together, ate together. Because we were always in new places, we only had each other. When our troupe director stole from us and ruined us, everyone had somewhere to go and someone to go with, except—her. I would never have brought her here, not with the master being the way he is, but—she—Marthe—thought of the disguise." He shook his head slowly, mourn-fully. "Tonette, I appeal to your womanly sympathy. She—Marthe—is an orphan. If she is exposed, she will be cast out. Or ruined. Or both."

Unseen by him, Tonette's lip trembled, but when she spoke, her voice was harsh. "Have I not already said I will keep her secret, if she will help with Sabine? I may have suffered exactly the fate you would spare Marthe, but I still have my honor of sorts. My word is my word. And to show my good faith, I will warn you, Bertrand—Marthe is in a danger you do not suspect."

"Tell me," he pleaded. "Who threatens her?"

"She threatens herself. She is in love with the Englishman."

"I know it," uttered Bertrand, barely audible.

"You may want to preserve her virtue, and she may have wanted to do so herself—until now—but love will blind her. *Is* blinding her. If you are not careful, she will offer herself to him, and then...well! And then she may as well have succumbed to Tremblay, because at least the master has the means to be generous, as long as his attention lasts." Tonette's mouth twisted in bitter memory. "But that Ezzwort, he has nothing but his pleasant looks and nice manner. He does not mean evil, but one does not always have to mean evil to do it. And when his year is done, he will be gone, leaving her nothing."

Bertrand's head had dropped into his hands. "Yes, yes. You are right. I believe you. He is a good young man, but he is a young man all the same. And I...thank you for your warning. You have a generous heart, madame, though you try to hide it."

At this she straightened, and there was a look almost of fear in her currant eyes. But though Tonette had never acted on the stage, she hid her expression as well as she could, arranging her face in its usual lines before he turned again to her.

"I do not know if I can save her," he confessed. "She has a warm heart. If I tell her to avoid him and forget him, I do not know if she will obey. I do not know if she *can*. She will tell me how good he is."

"He *is* good, for a man," Tonette cut him off shortly. "Which is why you will have to place the obstacle with him, I suppose."

"What do you mean? How can I place an obstacle?"

She pressed her lips together, thinking. "It is no use saying she is any sort of relation to you, even your daughter. And to admit she is not related at all—! No, monsieur, I am sorry to tell you that the only way to put an end to his consideration of her will be to tell him that she either *is* or *has been* your mistress. Do not look like that! You must think clearly about this. A man like Ezzwort will be fastidious about such things because I suspect he has never kept a mistress before. Had he had ten of them, even that would not serve." Springing up, she extended a hand to him. "Come now—chin up. You say you are an actor? You can carry this off because you know so much depends on it. Go find Ezzwort before Marthe does. Start with the *office* because Raulin will be hunting every person down."

Sleepwalker-like, Bertrand rose, and Tonette brushed his lapels and gave him a bracing pat on the chest. In a dim recess of his mind, he noted that he rather liked being fussed over by a woman. And Tonette—when he had walked away, gave herself a firm shake. "Don't be a fool, girl. One man is as bad as another. Why should you pat that one, just for staying true to his dead wife and for his care of this Marthe? Sentiment is for imbeciles."

CHAPTER 15

I was the more deceived.
— Shakespeare, *Hamlet*, III.i.1813 (c.1599)

The *office* of the house kitchens clamored with staff, and Raulin stood upon a chair to make himself heard. "We have two days to prepare. Any men who might be seen in the grand courtyard or anywhere within the house must wear livery. If you have none, Babeau is making a list. All women are to wear black, if they do not have dark green. Anyone who is not presentable or whose work is unseen can expect to have additional tasks and to submit to them without complaint. We will send to the *bureau d'addresse* for additional workers. And finally, if you have not yet paid your *capitation*, it must be given to Tollemer by tomorrow morning. Any questions?"

A swell of them, as well as indignation, complaint, and excitement swallowed the steward, but Bertrand paid no attention. He and Ezzwort had caught sight of each other in the gathering, and as soon as they were able, they pushed and angled their way together.

"I must speak to you at once," they announced in unison.

Charles smiled, but Bertrand's face was carved from stone.

"Will you come up to the schoolroom?" Charles suggested.

His quarters had never looked more cozy. The boys' chairs stood askew from their table, books and slates and slate pencils neat on Pierre's side and *à tort ou à travers* on Georges'. His own desk was kept tidy by Marthe, with items lined up on the edge. On the wall the day's lesson. On the little table the day's flowers.

It was to the little table Bertrand stalked. He rapped once on its surface, setting the petals trembling, before turning and striking his chosen attitude, one hand on his hip and the other upraised, finger pointing to the ceiling

"M. Ezzwort, it has come to my attention that you have worked to charm my—Marthe—from me."

"That is precisely what I wish to speak to you about," replied Charles, not properly daunted by the upraised finger and approaching him eagerly. "I must know everything about her, Bertrand. She is not your great-aunt, but what relation is she? Because I have learned—I know for a fact—she is younger than she pretends to be."

Distracted from his purpose, Bertrand flailed a moment. "What do you mean, you know for a fact?"

Charles hesitated. Not knowing if Marthe was the man's sister, cousin, sister-in-law, or similar such, he did not want to confess to kissing her straight off. "I know because—some of the paste she uses to disguise her true appearance—got on my hands."

Then Bertrand's consternation was genuine. "'Got on your hands,' sirrah! How should anything on my Marthe's face come to be on your hands? Have you been committing some outrage against her?"

"I do not mean to be," answered Charles gravely, deciding it were better to show his cards. "Sir, I ask again your relation to Marthe because I wish to—I wish to offer for her."

Bertrand sputtered a minute, the upraised hand faltering and flapping helplessly at the window and wall before taking hold of the neck of the vase. "*Offer?* Offer for *Marthe?*"

"I know it would be a long while before we could marry," admitted Charles. "I would need to complete my year here and then trust to a change in my family's fortunes or further employment of my own before I could afford to support us or get us to England, but I wanted you—and Marthe—to know my intentions are honorable."

His speech, astonishing as it was to Bertrand, was long enough for the seasoned actor to regain his footing. "I cannot believe my ears! You—" the pointing finger revived "—who not a fortnight ago made love to my young niece, the late Miss Martineau!"

The tutor's face darkened. "I know it. I do not deny it. But nor do I deny that I have felt a growing—affection for Marthe at the same time. All along. Not an affection of an amorous nature—that is, until now—but an affection all the same."

Bertrand gave the roar ordinarily earmarked for his performance of Eteocles, King of Thebes. "You openly admit that you favored both at the same time? And having pursued my niece, you now propose to do the same to my— my—my—"

"Your—" prompted Charles.

And then, like a man faced with an overlarge chunk of stew beef, Bertrand managed to swallow his scruples and proclaim, "My mistress! Marthe is indeed younger than I, but has been, for this past year my mistress! Of course she wears a disguise, and it was enough to keep away the master, but evidently not a hardened libertine such as yourself."

"Your mistress?" Charles doubled as if he had received a blow to the gut, taking hold of the corners of the boys' table. So stunned was he by this revelation that the insulting name Bertrand applied to him failed to register. "It cannot be true."

"Of course it can be true. And is."

"But she—"

Bertrand raised a knowing brow. "But she kissed you? What of it? Marthe kisses a lot of people."

At this the young Englishman straightened sharply and looked like he would have struck Bertrand, had he been the sort of man in the habit of violence.

"I am sure you thought she cared for you," the older man twisted the knife. "But how do you think we come to be together? She too is an actress. How could she have made her living on the stage, if she could not pretend love for every Éraste, Dorante and Astyanax?"

Charles could not say why he felt so heartsick. Had he not just worked to persuade himself to do the honorable thing with Marthe? Ought he not to feel perversely relieved that he was not expected to marry a woman of indeterminate years who had acted on the stage?

"Then she and Miss Martineau were..."

"Were what?" gulped Bertrand. *Ciel!* He should have

said Marthe was the mistress of the robes. The Suard of the troupe!

"Were they rivals for roles?" Charles pursued. "Is that why there was...something...between them, and Miss Martineau did not seem keen to be with Marthe?"

"Yes. They despised each other," replied Bertrand promptly. "It made things awkward for me at times, torn between mistress and niece. But never mind that. Jeanne is no more, of course." He crossed himself. "The more important point, Ezzwort, is that, if you think Marthe fond of you, she is only pretending."

"But why would she make such a show? She does not seem the sort to make fools of people."

"My dear Ezzwort, if you were—five-and-thirty and worked as a humble chambermaid, when you had been used to the colorful and variable life of a traveling actor, would you not seek amusement where you could?"

Five-and thirty? *Five-and-thirty.*

"But she can pronounce some English words," Charles persisted, knowing he sounded pitiable. "And she gave a similar family history to Miss Martineau's."

"It does not make her my aunt, Ezzwort," replied Bertrand patiently. "And where do you think she thought of those little details? From Jeanne herself." The footman ran a finger over the surface of the little table and held it up for inspection. "At least Marthe cleans passably. Alas, my Marthe is a wretched flirt, but I hope you will respect our prior relationship, monsieur, until such time as she chooses to end it."

Charles drew a long breath. "If you mean, will I please cease kissing her, I...will. I meant no offense."

Bertrand's smile was genuine, and he strode to the tutor's side to clap him by the shoulders. "I know it. You are a decent fellow. But now there is no more time to speak. Raulin has tasks for us all before the banquet, and you had better be fitted for your livery."

"*ET VOILÀ.*" Jeanne stepped back and regarded the slender stripling before her. "You will do, 'Armand.' In this household, no one will pay much attention to a boy of your age, especially one with your spots. Take care not to rub them."

"Yes," said Tonette, inspecting her sister Sabine. "Rubbing your face will reveal all." She threw Jeanne an arch glance, which the latter bore with chin raised.

"I wish I did not have to make my debut on such an important night," confessed Sabine.

"Bah! Raulin will take one look at your face and post you by some darkened doorway," Tonette assured her. You will not have to do a thing but stand there."

"If you have difficulty or questions," Jeanne told her, "you have only to ask Bertrand. Older man, distinguished, looks like a king. It is one of his wigs you are borrowing. He is like a father to me and can be trusted."

"Thank you," said Sabine, "but I had better not. Tonette told me to trust no man here."

But then, to the amazement of her auditors, Tonette said grudgingly, "No, it is true. You may trust Bertrand. He is...not so bad. But stay away from everyone else, if you can help it. They are birds of a feather."

"That isn't so!" cried Jeanne. "Sabine, the tutor M. Ellsworth is also a good man, and you may ask him for help as well."

At this suggestion Tonette only raised an infuriating brow.

"He *is*," Jeanne insisted. "He has been nothing but a friend to me."

"Now, now, *calme-toi*, Marthe. M. Ezzwort is a much younger man than good Bertrand, which means he still has plenty of chances to disappoint you." Tonette tapped Sabine's shoulder. "Let's go and present you, 'Armand.' Raulin should be enough out of his mind that you will pass."

IT WAS no easy task for Jeanne to find M. Ellsworth that afternoon. He was neither in his quarters nor the *office*. Everyone was fearfully busy rushing to and fro, fetching and carrying, barking orders and bewailing woes, therefore no one regarded her except to hiss at her to get out of the way, for heaven's sake. Jeanne even crept around the *garderobe* and stables in her search.

But when M. Ellsworth finally crossed her path, passing through the *porte* into the grand courtyard, she nearly overlooked him, and it was only the abrupt stiffening of his posture that made her glance back.

"Monsieur!"

"Marthe."

The coolness of his tone checked her. *He has come to his senses,* she thought. *He is ashamed of having kissed ugly old Marthe.*

Humbly she approached him. "I did not recognize you in livery."

"I daresay a lot of us are unrecognizable at present."

"Is there...anything I can do for you, monsieur?"

"Haven't you already done enough?"

She could not bear it—his cold disgust. If it would have

helped, she would have knelt on the paving stones to ask his forgiveness, but perhaps that would only increase his contempt.

Still, she edged one step nearer, so that her next words were barely audible. "Monsieur. I will forget everything that happened and never refer to it again. I knew it was madness. That you could never—want anything—from such a person as Marthe."

His own reply was equally low, but the *sang-froid* was gone. "How can you say that? Do you think I am such a one —that I would—touch you—for my own amusement? No, lady. Is that not rather your *modus operandi*?"

She raised anguished eyes to him then. "I do not understand. You are angry."

"Do you not amuse yourself with me, Marthe? You, who are another man's mistress?"

This accusation rendered her speechless, and the innocence of her expression only tore him further. "I do not know who you are, in truth. Not your age, not your story, not your—" he gestured at the whole of her "—not anything. But I do know you—belong to Bertrand. He told me. Excuse me now. I—Raulin has summoned those who are footmen tonight."

And then, before Jeanne managed to separate or articulate any of the thousand questions or words of explanation and indignation choking her, he was gone.

CHAPTER 16

But though this combat points me out a grave,
the Glory of this choice doth swell me up with a just pride.
— Pierre Corneille, *Horace*, II.i.377-378, trans. Sir Wm
Lower (1656)

The night of the Abbé Teray's banquet at the Hôtel de Tremblay would live in the memory of those present until those present were no more.

Before catastrophe struck, things were already headed sharply downwards. Everyone was irate. From Tollemer at Tremblay's side arranging invitations and issuing orders, to Barbe laboring in the scullery scrubbing unprecedented stacks and piles of cooking wares, to Yves grumbling that not a blossom nor a fruit would remain in his gardens, all was commotion. Complaints flew at the short notice they had been given, to prepare for something so momentous. Did the master think such things arranged themselves? That twenty extra hands and ten extra courses of unparalleled delicacy could be conjured from nothing? That the rooms through which the Abbé would pass and the *grande salle à manger* itself could be decked with enough flowers and lit with enough candles that one would think it was June? Yes, Raulin managed to press into service every idle person he could find lying in the gutters of Paris, and yes, it was fortunate that just at this time Tonette's younger brother Armand arrived looking for work, but even still it was all hands to the pump. The English tutor and even hideous Marthe must be made to fetch and carry, though Raulin growled to Louise that she must part with one of her dresses for the night, because Marthe was bad enough, without creeping about in one of her fusty old gowns. Louise screamed in protest that nothing in her wardrobe would ever be touched by any smelly old hunchback, but so plagued and harrassed was Raulin that he thundered, threatened, roared—and carried his point.

Things began well enough. When the Abbé's coach drew up at the open gate, both *Suisses* were there to look stone-faced and magnificent. The servants were drawn up two-deep in the grand court, like limes flanking an avenue, with the handsomest in front and the less presentable well hidden. Both because of his good looks and because Tremblay wanted to display the humbling position in which he had placed the Englishman, Charles headed the line of attractive footmen. He kept his gaze lowered, but was surprised into glancing up when the Abbé paused and asked of Tremblay, "This is the one?"

"Yes, Monseigneur." Earlier in his career, in a visit to Versailles, Tremblay had mistakenly addressed the Abbé Terray as "Père Abbot" and been roundly ridiculed. It had been La Pompadour herself who informed him, "Despite his tonsure, my friend is no practicing priest, monsieur.

When you address him thus, you seem to mock." Thus humiliated, Tremblay did not dare open his mouth again for some time, but he did observe the address those beneath the Abbé's rank used.

Abbot Joseph Marie Terray, controller-general of finances for all France, studied Charles leisurely from head to foot, one eyebrow lifting. Then, with a "Well done there," he passed on.

Swelling with satisfaction, Tremblay marched away beside his honored guest, which was why the first crack in the façade went unnoticed by him.

But a mere moment later, the footman beside Charles gave a low groan, drawing the attention of those nearest. Paul had been given the task of fetching supplementary cakes and sweets and pastries from the pâtissier Stohrer that day, and, as a strapping fellow much beloved by the female kitchen staff, he was further encouraged to sample generously and repeatedly the rich items being prepared for the banquet. The result of this excessive gourmandizing was a red face and dyspepsia. No sooner did the master and the Abbé climb the steps and enter the vestibule, than Paul shoved Charles aside and hurtled across the courtyard to be ill in one of Yves' potted plants. A great frenzy followed, punctuated by finger-pointing and hissed accusations. No one thought to help up Paul from the paving stones, and Raulin went so far as to kick the greedy lad before whirling on the liveried onlookers.

"You!" he thrust a finger in Charles' chest. "You must take Paul's place in the serving duties."

"But I have never served," Charles said, his voice more surprised than defensive. "Which is why you told me I would only have to stand by doors and, when handed something, hand it onward to someone who knew what he was doing."

"Never mind what I said earlier. Now you must take Paul's place. Do whatever Gregoire and Émile and Chapone do." With a sneer he added, "I presume if you have not served before, you have yourself been *served*? And you there —boy—what was your name again?"

"Do you mean me?" gasped Sabine, pointing like an idiot to herself. "A-Armand."

"Well, A-Armand, you are now a second footman, in place of Ezzwort. Bah! Cannot you wash your face or something? Your eruptions will make Monseigneur the Abbé want to be sick as Paul."

"I cannot help my pimples," mumbled Sabine.

"Stupid child!" Raulin growled. "Starting tomorrow we will put you on a diet of vegetables with no sauce and bread with no butter, but for tonight keep your head down and talk to no one."

Sabine was only too happy to comply, and she bobbed a curtsey by accident, which then had to be disguised as a crouch, as if she were limbering to carry heavy trays. The steward rolled his eyes, his mind already on the next problem to be solved, and hardly had he turned than it was before him.

"Where is Louise?" he demanded, his eye running up and down the line of maids as if they had conspired to hide her. "Mme de Louviers' carriage will arrive next, and Louise was to attend to her."

Calm in the face of the storm, Tonette stepped forward. "Louise is unwell."

"She did not like giving Marthe her dress," added another maid mischievously, "and says the master will agree with her, when she has a chance to tell him, so she has taken to her bed."

"Louise is a fool," the steward cursed, "if she does not know her power over him is fading, and this will do away with it altogether. But there is nothing to be done tonight. You will take her place, Tonette."

"Yes, sir. But what of the tea I was meant to serve after supper?"

"Imogene must take that."

"But sir, I was to tend the lesser ladies' needs and wants," whined Imogene. "Surely I cannot be expected to do both."

"Tend? Tend what?" snapped Raulin. "What will they need, besides a shawl fetched or something mended or a stain cleaned? Marthe will have to do that, and you will have to serve the tea. We cannot have someone as ugly as Marthe serving tea to the master's guests."

This promotion of Marthe evoked universal dismay. Marthe! Marthe, possibly to be seen by any of the guests? This would be the end of the Hôtel de Tremblay's renown! But the steward could stand no more, not with Mme de Louviers and the other guests at the very gate.

"Bertrand," he said therefore, "go find your hag of a great-aunt and tell her to make herself as little repellant as possible in so short a time. She will have the dress from Louise. Make her do something with her hair and dunk her in a barrel of *eau de cologne* if need be. No excuses!"

BERTRAND HAD time only to shout Raulin's instructions up to Jeanne before he must take up his station, but her head appeared at the top of her ladder, and her furious face and unscrolled tresses sent a shudder down him, as if he faced the Medusa.

"Why did you tell M. Ellsworth that despicable lie?" she hissed, batting aside the orders he delivered. "He will be ice and stone to me now!"

"It was for your own protection, Jea—Marthe! I will explain it to you tomorrow, but you must fix yourself and come down at once to the *grande salle*. Be as presentable a Marthe as you can, and I will see you shortly."

When he was gone, Marthe fell back on her lumpy mattress. That was all Bertrand could say? It was "for her own protection"? Did no one see, as she did, that no protection was needed from so honorable a gentleman as M. Ellsworth? What use was protecting the reputation of a mere actress and chambermaid, when she had already lost something more vital, something irreplaceable? For M. Charles Ellsworth now owned her heart. He need never return her love, need never kiss her again (so she swore to herself), much less marry her, if only she might stay near him the rest of her life as his friend and servant. Yes, let her only be with him, in Paris or the ends of the earth, if life took him there. It would be enough.

It *would*. It would have to be.

Indeed, he need never promise her anything, but she, Jeanne Martineau, married herself to him in this moment.

She sat up, pressing both hands to her heart. Yes. She married herself to him. And like all good vows, this one must be cemented by a sacrifice. The Jeanne Martineau in her must die in truth, leaving behind only Marthe Collet, with her five-and-thirty years, her supposed lost virtue, and her lined face.

"Very well," Jeanne murmured, taking up her recovered blue wool dress, flung down by a spiteful Louise hours earlier. "*Adieu,* Jeanne. But if you must go, tonight will be your last appearance, if only as a ghost, half-unseen."

THE FIGURES which glided and gathered and gossiped in the Hôtel de Tremblay's *grande salle* were more elegant than the usual throng of bourgeois and humble petitioners calling to dispute their tax bills. Hired musicians sawed away in a corner. By the massive marble fireplace at the head of the room, the Abbé held court, clad in dark-grey velvet and ivory brocade, the whiteness of his tiewig impeccable. Tremblay hung on his every word, while his mother favored the controller-general with a fixed and rouged grin frightening to behold, setting her pug down to trot about, as a sign that the great man held her full attention. Raulin anchored a corner, balefully regarding the movements of the troops under him. A pair of footmen beside every door. Maids waiting behind screens or outside doorways (he assumed), prepared for a beckoning nod or cross look to summon assistance. Perhaps, just perhaps, despite stupid Paul and recalcitrant Louise, the evening would come off smoothly, Raulin thought. If something went wrong in the kitchens, Tollemer would fall upon Babeau and Cavaliere, but Raulin cared nothing for that, so long as Tollemer did not fall upon him. Yes, by this time tomorrow, Tollemer might be summoning him to the *cabinet* to say, "Raulin, though you were given insufficient time to prepare and though such heavy burdens were placed upon you, you nevertheless surpassed yourself. Therefore the master and I have agreed you should have—"

It was at this point in his daydream that reality intruded. Mme de Louviers crooked a finger toward the door leading to the antechamber. And like a loosely, inexpertly knit garment, it took but that one tiny tug on a dangling yarn to unravel the whole.

Mme de Louviers, as noted, spied a tiny rent in the hem of her petticoat from where she trod upon it in ascending the steps to the vestibule. She beckoned the maid, but Tonette had just been called away by Bertrand. For no sooner had Mme Tremblay's wretched pug been set free than it piddled in a corner of the room, to the delight and horror of the guests. That left Jeanne to respond to Mme de Louviers' summons. Taking a deep breath, she lurched out in her (swiftest) Marthe hobble, eyes lowered and sewing housewife in hand.

And every member of the Tremblay household took a sharp breath.

Because—was this Marthe?—Of course it must be she —hunched and limping, but with a peculiar grace, as if the steps were those of a dance. Marthe, clad in a becoming blue wool *robe à l'anglaise* which fit as if it were tailored for her, apart from some tightness where it pressed upon her hump. Even the hump was not as large as they had imagined it under the ill-fitting rags she usually wore. Indeed, apart from that deformity, she had rather a pretty figure! A pretty figure? Humpbacked Marthe? And though she kept her gaze on the floor, each wondered if he had really got a clear look at her before this point, for her countenance, though lined and not fashionably rosy, boasted undeniably regular, non-loathsome features. And Marthe's hair, which heretofore had been stuffed under a limp, ruffled servant's cap, with only those grizzled locks emerging, was now dressed as Raulin had commanded. It was neither so high and blue-powdered as Mme Tremblay's, nor studded with birds and flowers and ribbons as Mme de Louviers', but neither was any of it false. Pinned over a modest cushion, Marthe's hair was clearly thick and curling and every inch her own.

Standing on the left-hand side of the door of the vestibule, Charles thought he might never breathe again. His confusion threatened to overwhelm him. The blue dress, the curling hair, the graceful movements—it was as if Miss Martineau's specter floated before him. He knew Marthe's hump was false; he knew her paint hid her true complexion and age. But, if she was not Jeanne Martineau herself, she must surely, surely be the young lady's relation. It could not be otherwise. Her older sister? Older cousin? Aunt?

He knew one thing in that moment: he did not care if she were Bertrand's mistress. He did not care if she had flirted with a dozen men. Did not care if her kindnesses were dispensed to all and sundry—if kisses such as she had given him were scattered as easily as flower petals. He only knew at that moment that he loved her. He loved her, and there was no pride left to him.

All this took place in the space of that one common breath, and then three things happened simultaneously.

Bertrand appeared from nowhere, pulling Tonette by the hand to deposit her at Mme de Louviers' feet.

Charles stepped forward to—do what? Call to Marthe? Embrace her?

And lastly, Sabine staggered up the vestibule steps bearing a heavy tureen of soup which she prayed she could carry all the way to the *salle à manger* without having to set it down to catch her breath.

It turned out she was relieved of her burden in a different manner altogether, for, as she heaved both it and herself into the *grande salle*, she collided with the moving

Charles. He being so much bigger, the impact sent her careering forward, the tureen flying from her grasp. It sailed for a timeless instant through the air, a winter moon tracing an arc of silver through the night sky before setting —abruptly—on the marble floor with a *bong* both deep and liquid. From within the tureen, Cavaliere's excellent consommé then swung out in one shining wave. It paused briefly, as if to ensure it had the room's undivided attention, before showering its golden bounty generously, abundantly, thoroughly, and unavoidably upon the helpless Mme de Louviers.

Instinctively Jeanne had drawn back, one of her beautiful hands flying in horror to her mouth, but it sounded as if every other mouth in the room was open and screaming. Sabine screamed in a manner that would have given her disguise away, had anyone been in a position to notice her. Mme de Louviers screamed (and then choked on the consommé running down her face). Mme Tremblay screamed, a scream which too quickly metamorphosed into a hysterical cackle.

Raulin never knew how he got across the room, but the next moment he was there, slipping in the consommé and grabbing, panicked, for something to break his fall. That something turned out to be Mme de Louviers sopping overskirt, which was of such fine brocade that it did not rend in the least but instead provided a sturdy handle by which Raulin pulled her over atop him.

Mme Tremblay's cackle became a whoop, but her son hastened as quickly as he could, taking care to avoid the wet floor, where Sabine and Charles and Jeanne and Tonette had dropped to their knees, using anything and everything to absorb the soup. Crimson with fury, Tremblay hauled Mme de Louviers upright and gave Tonette a kick. "See to madame."

"Get away from me all of you!" cried Mme de Louviers, one hand supporting her leaning hair, the running paint on her face giving her the appearance of a melted candle. "I want none of you clumsy imbeciles touching me!"

It was Mme Tremblay's Solange who took charge of the angry woman, marching her out of the room, while her mistress finally managed to school her expression. The dowager then rose as if such things happened at every fine banquet in France. She extended an arm to the Abbé. "Monseigneur, if you would lead us in to dinner, I believe they are ready for us. I am sorry there will be no soup course."

Straightening his frock coat with a jerk, Tremblay pinned a smile on his face and raised his arms to his guests. "Please, please, ignore the fracas and follow madame. What can one do? The servants in Paris are so bad…"

But as the guests obeyed and began to shuffle out, now laughing and throwing looks over their shoulders, the master turned back to Raulin. "See to this," he snarled, "or I will see to you!" Then his hand flew out to snatch Jeanne by the wrist. "And you, *chère* Marthe—you are to come to my quarters tonight and wait for me." Lifting one finger, Tremblay drew it in a deliberate stroke down her cheek, inspecting the grey smear it left. "It seems you have played me for a fool, but no longer. Tonight." He flung her arm away, spun on his heel, and followed his guests.

"I will kill you, stupid boy!" roared Raulin, the second the heavy doors to the dining room closed. Wild-eyed, he seized Sabine and shook her by the shoulders until her teeth rattled.

"Here, stop that," ordered Charles, thrusting an arm

between them. "It was not Armand's fault. I ran into him like an ox."

"Nor was it your fault!" insisted Jeanne, tugging on Ellsworth's sleeve and dispensing with her old-and-crippled act altogether. "It was an accident, Raulin."

"Accident?" bellowed the steward. "I never saw such a collection of incompetents! Boy, you are dismissed. Pack your things at once and never let me see you again!"

"He is my brother!" protested Tonette. "Please, Raulin, you cannot dismiss him. He is young. He will learn."

"It was not his fault, Raulin," repeated Charles.

"I don't care!" roared the steward. "I know whose fault it most certainly was not—*mine*! Therefore, if someone must pay, it will be him."

His jaw tightening, Charles took a deep breath. "Raulin, if the boy goes, I go too."

"And I," vowed Jeanne.

"You must go, in any case," Charles told her, his voice urgent. "You cannot stay here to let the master accost you."

"Nor do I intend to!"

"Neither of you can go anywhere," the steward jeered. "You, Ezzwort, are stuck here because of the two hundred livres you owe the master. And you, 'Marthe,' whoever you are, must stay because, without male protection or a roof over your head, you will end in a brothel or the depths of the Seine in a week."

"She has my protection," declared Bertrand, inserting himself. "And she and I will indeed go before I let that man —the master—lay a hand on her."

"Is that so? Where will you go, I wonder? And with what money?"

"Well—I—er—we—" fumbled Bertrand.

"Just as I thought," said Raulin.

But Bertrand seized Marthe's hand. "Nevertheless, we go. We have a little, between us."

"Bertrand. Marthe. Wait," Charles interjected. His pulse sped, and he thought his heartbeat must be heard by every person in the *grande salle*. "Listen to me. Marthe, before you leave with Bertrand—there is something I must say. Something I must tell you. I cannot deny it any longer."

She raised glowing dark eyes to his. Then he would speak to her? He would not freeze her out because of the lies he had been told?

"Yes, monsieur?"

"Marthe. I—I have nothing to offer you," Charles said. "Nothing at all, at present, of-of-of a material nature. But what I have is yours. I mean to say—my heart. I have my heart, and it is yours."

Color flooded her face, so rich it showed beneath the layer of paste. "Your *heart,* monsieur?" Her voice was thick. For one moment Charles thought she would hurl herself into his arms, but with a struggle she shrunk back. "Ah. But —M. Ellsworth, you cannot love me. You do not know who I am."

"I know enough." Trepidations filled him, but he had gone too far for retreat, even if he wanted to. And he did not want to. Whoever she was, it was too late for him. "I offer you my heart," he repeated. "It is yours altogether, Marthe."

"Though I am five and thirty?" she whispered.

"...Yes."

"And though you think me Bertrand's mistress?"

A gasp rose from those within hearing, but neither Jeanne nor Charles remarked it.

"Yes," he said again. "If you will only...give him up and be true to me."

209

"I would do it," she murmured. "But—how can you say you love me, when I am...so ugly?"

"But...*are* you?" he mused. He drew out his handkerchief and wetted it along a chair arm with consommé. "If you are, you are. But may I please see your face as it is?"

Slowly, like one under a spell, she took the cloth from him and began to rub her face, carefully and thoroughly. Cavaliere's consommé worked as well as any lotion, and when she could feel her bare flesh tingling with the contact and with exposure, she shut her eyes a moment.

Then she looked up.

The shock which had met her claim to be Bertrand's mistress was nothing compared to the outburst following this new revelation. Everyone spoke at once; everyone crowded; everyone questioned her and Bertrand and each other. But Charles simply stared.

"Speak to me," pleaded Jeanne, as she was jostled.

"But—who are you?" he managed. "You look like—but how can you be...Miss Martineau?"

"Yes! It is I! I am Miss Martineau. I am Jeanne! Forgive us, M. Ellsworth, for our deception! We would not—*I* would not have disguised myself, but for Tremblay—" she spat the name. "I wanted to tell you! A hundred times I wanted to tell you. And I am sorry we made you think she was dead—we did not know what else to do because I came face to face with Tremblay that day in the Tuileries, and he told Bertrand to summon me at once—But I hated to make you sad," she insisted. "Forgive us. Forgive *me*. Please, M. Ellsworth—don't be angry."

At some point her hands were in his, and he was clutching them so tightly she couldn't feel her fingers. She feared an explosion of rage and recrimination, but he was making soothing sounds. "Shhh...I understand. I understand. I...am only too glad you are still alive, dear, dear Miss Martineau."

Relief made her tremulous, but a wavering dimple appeared. "Oh...*vraiment*? Now truly it is 'dear, dear Miss Martineau'? Tell me, sir, to whom did you offer your heart a minute ago? Have you forgotten Marthe, now that Jeanne has returned?"

"It is a fair question," he conceded. "And one I am not certain I can answer yet because I am still amazed. I must learn who Marthe and Jeanne truly are."

"Then you retract your offer?"

"I do not. I cannot. It is too late. It seems I love both of you and neither of you and all of you. Please, Miss Martineau, do not leave me in suspense. I beg you to accept my heart and, along with it, my protection."

The teasing glint in her eyes faded. "Your protection?" she repeated. "You ask me then to be your mistress?"

"No, Marthe—Jeanne, rather." Heedless of the puddles of consommé, Charles sank to one knee. "Jeanne, I ask you to be my wife. It would mean a life of poverty here, while I find work to repay my debt, and then it would mean going to England when I could afford to get us there. And any marriage we contract here would not stand at home, so you would not be my wife in England's eyes until we were married there, but you would be my wife in the eyes of the Catholic church and in the eyes of God."

"Don't believe him," advised Tonette. "Unless you intend to be his mistress. That is what all that rigmarole means."

"That is not what it means!" declared Jeanne, wheeling on her. "I am sorry you have suffered in the past, but you must not judge all men by that monster Tremblay. It is true the master is a beast, and so are *you*—" jabbing a finger at

Raulin's chest "—and so might be all the other men you have encountered, Tonette, but M. Ellsworth is an exception as much as Bertrand!" Turning back to the tutor, she breathed, "You ask me to marry you, M. Ellsworth?"

"Call me Charles, my dearest love."

"You ask me to marry you, Charles? I say Yes. I say Yes, with all my heart. Even if we leave the Hôtel de Tremblay tonight to sleep in the streets, and even if you cannot marry me in England's eyes for—years and years, I say Yes."

The next moment they were in each other's arms, heedless of damp clothing, their audience and Raulin's protests.

"I say you can go nowhere, Ezzwort!" he blazed. "I cannot stop this—this Marthe-Jeanne person from going, but if you stir from this place, Tollemer and the master will arrest you for debt."

"*I* shall be responsible for Ezzwort's debt," pronounced Bertrand. Stepping forth, he thumped his chest as he did when playing Horace confronting his wife's brother Curiace.

"Your young mistress deserts you for another man, and you wish to take on your rival's debt?" mocked Tonette, even while Jeanne cried, "You haven't the money, Bertrand!" To Tonette she added, "I was never his mistress —that was something he made up."

"That was something *I* made up," corrected Tonette archly. But Jeanne had already been swept anew into Ellsworth's embrace, his hands cradling her face again so that she did not hear Bertrand say, "You are like a daughter to me, *ma chère*, and therefore it is only fitting I supply your dowry, in the form of paying M. Ezzwort's debt. I will have Tollemer draw up the promissory note and sign my name to it. You will go with my blessing."

This time it was Charles who pulled away to say,

"Bertrand, how can I thank you? I promise you that I will write *you* a promissory note and send you regular payments from England."

Raulin gave an impatient scoff. "You're all a passel of fools if you think Tollemer or the master will accept a promissory note from Bertrand here, with nothing to offer as security."

"He will not need security," declared Tonette in ringing tones which would have done her credit on the stage of the Tuileries theatre. "He will not need security because I myself will pay Tremblay *in full*, and M. Ezzwort will write his promissory note to *me*."

This announcement fell upon the company like a bombshell and was sufficiently astonishing that even Charles and Jeanne loosened their grip on each other to gape at her.

"But why—"

"Madame, why would you—"

"What is so wondrous?" she stared them down, crossing her arms under her bosom. "I never thought again to meet any man deserving the name of 'gentleman,' much less two—" Here her voice trembled, and she quickly cleared her throat. "I have the money. Why should I not play moneylender? Bertrand, you have the gallantry, but not the means, so let me supply them."

"But it is not gallantry if I do not pay!" he objected. "She is *my* daughter, so I must pay."

"You haven't twenty livres, much less two hundred, whether I am your daughter or not," Jeanne pointed out practically. "Therefore, I am sorry to agree with Raulin, but you cannot pay, dear Bertrand."

"Let her be my daughter as well, then," suggested Tonette quietly.

"What do you mean?" Bertrand demanded.

Humbly, she bowed her head before him. "I mean only that, if you were willing, we might marry, and then she would be my daughter too."

Bertrand was speechless and Jeanne not much better. Sabine forgot herself entirely and sank with a squelching sound into the moist seat vacated by Mme de Louviers, and such was Raulin's distraction that he did not reprimand the new footman.

"You needn't decide straight away," resumed Tonette, blushing. "I know you have never thought of a woman since you lost your wife, years and years ago. The offer of the loan is not dependent on your reply."

But something was already softening, even melting, in the lines of his noble visage, and Jeanne thought M. Heine, the former, dishonest managing director of their acting troupe, would not have believed his eyes to see the tears glisten in Bertrand's.

"It has been lonely," said he. "And a long, long time. It will be even lonelier without Jeanne."

"Then come," Tonette coaxed, taking hold of his sleeve. "Let our 'daughter' and 'son' have their freedom and each other. And you take me and my Sabine. Let us write the note and all be gone."

"You cannot go!" sputtered Raulin. "Who will clean up this mess? Who will serve the tea? What will the master say? What will Tollemer do to me?"

It was Sabine who answered him as the lovers drifted toward the door. Removing her bagwig and giving her head a good scratch, she grinned at him. "I'm afraid that is your problem, monsieur. But at least you will not have to suffer having me as a footman again. I hope I will be better at whatever I do next. *Adieu.*"

EPILOGUE

A deed may be avoided, by delivering it up to be cancelled;
that is to have lines drawn over it, in the form of lattice
work or *cancelli*; though the phrase is now used figuratively
for any manner of obliteration or defacing it.
— William Blackstone, *Commentaries on the laws of England*
(1767)

From Paris to Calais there were thirty posts, and at
each a tip of three *sols* must be paid, besides the
expense of the *carosse* itself, but Tonette had calcu-
lated their expenses to a nicety, dividing the money into
separate envelopes to be opened at each stage, and the
newlyweds (in the eyes of God and the Catholic church)
nestled happily in their corner, confident of the sufficiency
of their purse and talking in a jumble of French and English
to avoid the listening ears of their fellow passengers.

"How many years do you suppose it will take to pay her

back?" asked Jeanne, admiring her husband's straight nose and finely-modeled jaw.

"Oh, a hundred, perhaps," he teased. "But maybe only fifty if we are sparing. When I wrote to a former schoolmate from Winchester College about how I was tutoring Pierre and Georges, he mentioned hearing that our old mathematics master—who already seemed ancient when *we* were boys—now sleeps through his lessons. So perhaps there might be a position for me."

"I would adore that!" his wife cried. "Might I do something too, for all the schoolboys? I can cook and mend and —and do theatricals. Or teach French."

Charles laughed. "There is no French taught there, my love. Why do you think mine was so inadequate when we met? Winchester prefers its charges learn dead languages no one speaks. Therefore you had better do the theatricals. You certainly fooled me with your acting."

"Bah," said Jeanne. "I was terrible as Marthe from the moment you came. For I did not mind being old and foul and hunched until I met you. Then I could not bear it. Bit by bit, my disguise fell away as vanity prevailed."

"Thank heavens. Or I would have had to marry Marthe, hump and all."

"*Menteur!*" she accused, chuckling. "You lie, my dear. You might have kept Marthe as a pet, but I do not think you would have loved her until you discovered her hump was false."

"I don't know about that. I think if another week had gone by, I might have offered for her even if she donned her smelly shift again."

Her merry laugh made him want to kiss her, but with so many witnesses he settled for taking her hand.

"In my head and in my heart all was confusion,"

Charles went on, his gaze holding hers. "I was drawn by the elusive Miss Martineau from the moment I saw her on the Pont Royal, but who was more the phantom? She, or the changeling charmer I sensed in Marthe? Circumstances chose for me: Miss Martineau slipped further and further away until it seemed she had gone where I could not follow, but Marthe drew nearer and nearer."

Jeanne sighed with satisfaction, leaning to press her cheek against his shoulder. "Yes, I drew nearer and nearer. Oh, Charles—that day in the glasshouse! I thought I would die of happiness."

"Too bad Tonette scared your happiness out of you," he observed, having heard the story of Sabine's coming by this point. He rubbed his thumb along her gloved palm, but one glance around the coach showed him that more was not possible. Indeed, however little their companions understood what was said, they were satisfied to watch a dumb show of the beautiful couple.

"She might have scared my happiness away for that day, Charles, but you nearly banished it forever when you thought I was Bertrand's mistress!"

His mouth twisted ruefully. "Yes, that presented more of an obstacle than your painted wrinkles or crooked carriage. But I discovered I could resign myself to even *that*, if you could be persuaded to abandon him for me."

At this declaration, his wife pressed against his side most distractingly, and Charles did not think he could withstand temptation another moment. Would it really be so bad, to take Jeanne on his lap and kiss her senseless? They would likely never see these people again after Calais.

But the heavens themselves arranged the matter, for, at that juncture, a sudden downpour began to beat on the *carosse*, drawing cries of alarm from the other passengers.

The beefy blacksmith sprang up, struggling to shut the open window, while the rest of them offered clamorous advice and criticism.

The rest of them, save two.

The distraction was just long enough for Charles to press his lips against Jeanne's ripe ones for one hungry moment, and for his breath to shorten and her color to rise, before order was restored. Within the *carosse,* at least. What carnival reigned in the lovers' hearts was mercifully known only to themselves.

"We will be married again in London," he said. "I do not think I can bear to wait weeks for the banns to be read in Winchester."

"But Charles, how can we afford to stay in London several days? I am certain Tonette will not have provided for that."

"Open her last letter. The one that says, 'To be read on the boat to Dover.'"

Jeanne shook her head at him teasingly. "But we are not on the boat to Dover."

"Obey me, wife, or I will fetch the letter off your person myself, and our fellow passengers will put us out of the *carosse* for misbehavior."

Winking at him, she reached into the pocket of her cloak, withdrew the packet of letters, and untied the ribbon binding them. "Ooh—it's a good heavy one," she said, passing the letter to him.

The weight came not solely from the louis d'or which tumbled out and was snatched up by Jeanne to tuck in their precious purse. No. With a puzzled frown, Charles unfolded the second sheet enclosed.

He and Jeanne stared at each other, open-mouthed.

"*C'est le billet à ordre!*" she gasped, forgetting herself enough to say it in French.

It was indeed the promissory note. The very one drawn up on Charles' desk in the schoolroom for two hundred and thirty-seven livres: two hundred to repay Tremblay and thirty-seven to provide travel expenses back to England. Everything the parties agreed to, exactly as they remembered drawing it up.

But it was covered in hatched lines and across it in thick red letters was written, "*Annulée.*" Cancelled.

"Read the note," urged Jeanne. The combination of Tonette's script and her regional spelling was too much for Charles, however, and he gave it to her to translate.

"'My dear friends,'" she read. "'You will be surprised by what you find here, but please accept this gift, which I dared not mention until you were out of the country because I did not want you to fight me about it. The debt is nothing because the rumors of my "dowry" were true. I saved not only my wages but also the "hush-money" Tremblay provided when I was with child. As if anything could hush servants' wagging tongues!

"'I cancel this debt because you have given me the greater gifts: restored faith that good men exist and the best of men himself. I speak of Bertrand, of course. Therefore go with our blessings on your match. I hope, when I write to you again, with Bertrand I will call you my son and daughter. Tonette.'"

Charles gave a low whistle. "Can it be true?"

Jeanne's eyes glimmered with joyful tears. "Oh, Charles, of course it can! It is the perfect wedding gift—not just the debt being cancelled, but also Bertrand having Tonette and Sabine. How shall we thank her? Do you think, if we have daughters, we could name them Tonette and Sabine?"

"I'm not certain Sabine did anything besides spill soup on everyone," he chuckled.

"But of course she did!" argued Jeanne. "Sabine precipitated the crisis."

He grinned at her. "And if we have boys...? Bertrand and Antoine? Or do we give up and call them Pierre and Georges?"

But Jeanne was fingering the cancelled promissory note thoughtfully. "Look at this—I never knew 'Bertrand Collet' was his stage name." She pointed to Bertrand's signature as the witness. "Benjamin Collet. All this time he was a Benjamin."

"Benjamin Collet and Tonette Austin," read Charles. "Benjamin and Austin. I rather like the sound of that. But maybe not so well as Tonette and Sabine. I would love two miniature Jeannes."

"And I would love two miniature Charleses."

Folding up the notes and returning them to her, he gathered her close. "Well, my charming Mrs. Ellsworth, we will have to see what the future holds."

The *Georgians in Paris* frolics continue with *A Match Gone Awry*!

She needs a match. He's here to help.

Desperate to leave Paris, Gabrielle d'Amilly has set her sights on an English diplomat who can whisk her away to a happier life. But when an attempt to catch his eye goes wrong, she enlists the British navy lieutenant Harvey Barlow to help in her scheme. Under the guise of visiting a friend, Lt Barlow arrives in Paris with the task of checking France's relations with the discontented colonies. Playing at matchmaking won't hurt his mission, especially for a good cause. But when his intentions to be helpful turn to feelings of love, he finds himself distracted from his duties. In his current position in the navy, he cannot give Gabrielle the happy life she's after. With war threatening, Harvey and Gabrielle are forced to decide to hold to their previous goals or strive for an imperfectly perfect match.

BOOKS IN THE GEORGIANS IN PARIS SERIES:

The Accidental Servants by Christina Dudley
A Match Gone Awry by Arlem Hawks
The Vicomte's Masquerade by Sofi Laporte
A Sham Betrothal by Jennie Goutet

Meet Charles and Jeanne again with their extended family in the Ellsworth Assortment series of Regency romances, beginning with their niece Florence's story in *Tempted by Folly*.

THE ELLSWORTH ASSORTMENT

Tempted by Folly
The Belle of Winchester
Minta in Spite of Herself
A Scholarly Pursuit
Miranda at Heart
A Capital Arrangement

THE HAPGOODS OF BRAMLEIGH

The Naturalist
A Very Plain Young Man
School for Love
Matchless Margaret
The Purloined Portrait
A Fickle Fortune

PRIDE AND PRESTON LIN

www.christinadudley.com